# THE
# POTION PEDDLER'S
# ALMANAC

## BY
## COLIN R. JAMES

CRESTINGWAVE
PUBLISHING

**THE POTION PEDDLER'S ALMANAC**

Published by

Cresting Wave Publishing, LLC
731 Yosemite Ave., Suite B322
Merced, California 95340

www.gocwpub.com

*"You buy a book. We plant a tree."*

ISBN: 978-0-9889048-5-9

# OH, FOR A MUSE OF FIRE...

## (Bill Shakespeare - *Henry V.*)

Not so much. More like inspiration from Mr. Becks and his twelve lovely daughters, always to be found loitering around the beer section of the local supermarket - waiting to be accosted by some lonely bastard with a long night ahead of him.

There's a word for *wanton beer-bottled femininity* and it's a word which I'm not prepared to use here. Not wishing to offend, but rather to inspire, I can advise the would-be novelist to sup deep and draw whatever wisdom it is that the thousands before us have sought at the bottom of multitudinous bottles.

If at first you don't succeed, then drink, drink again!

~ C J

# THE POTION PEDDLER

*England 1755...*

O'ER HILL AND DALE he rode, past moss-covered dry-stone walls and creeper-caught bridges, following the ancient roads hacked by Caesar's legions through the soft English chalk. Along coastal trails blazed by the retreating Saxon; twixt green bowers of gnarled spreading forests and across the wastes of stark deserted moorland, the grind of iron-shod wheels on greased axle trees.

Undeterred by wind and weather, the same ancient routes crossed and re-crossed to reach the vague familiarity of distant villages and time-worn market towns; the clip-clop of plodding diligence to fresh faces and familiar vistas.

A whale-oil lamp swung above the man in the hooded cloak, tapping its wooden tattoo on the side of the hooped caravan. The familiar clink of glass with every hoof fall; the slosh of liquids medicinal and the clatter of necessary instruments. The smell of horse was strong in his nostrils; the tang of pestled powder bitter on his tongue, the stain of dark paste upon his fingers.

He always broke camp at night, stealing away from candle-lit curiosity and the press of eager crowds. There was no point prolonging contact, garnering associations or establishing friendships. The exchange of hard-won silver for bottled miracles and manufactured tablets was oft regretted the morning after the night before. Dubious cures for infestations and arthritis; promised miracles to ease the burden of daily life only a palm-pressed sixpence away. His timekeeping was meticulous. Never outstay the welcome of a settlement more than once every few years.

Acquaintances kindled soon burnt. Familiarity bred contempt—as did the fact his potions were worthless. Snake oil and powdered Egyptian mummy, dried toad and unicorn horn infused the heady concoctions and broken promises that persuaded village folk to dig, eagerly, into leather purses.

Of an evening, when the crowds were gone and the campfire blazed, he would sit quietly, his hand coursing over velum, ink splashing in the firelight. The only sounds were of curb-chained horses cropping grass – the gleam of flame-lit brass. Recording the events of the day; penning for posterity the stories learned and experiences shared. New tales to relate to future customers – to expound upon, to embellish.

The art of potions wasn't in the mixture, nor in the voluminous recipes laid down by generations past; secrets divulged by father to son, from mother to daughter; forgotten knowledge retained by travelling folk and distributed frugally among those outside the inner circle. Although an initiate of the ancient rite of healers, the peddler knew that it took more than colored glass and powdered opiate to heal the body and excite the imagination.

His audience sought succor beyond the physical plane, thronging to his caravan in eager anticipation for both cure and enlightenment. Stories of adventure; tales of distant lands, dragon-slaying knights, daring deeds done by daring men.

Engaged in enigmatic conversation, it wasn't long before his product was crossing the counter to be scooped up by needy souls, weak in body and bereft of worldly contact.

Although tutored in the ways of healing, it was a story-teller's heart that he possessed.

# DIVINE INTERVENTION

*England 1984...*

ROGER STOPPED THE CAR and turned off the engine. There were only four collections due today. He should be finished by ten, giving him more than enough time to skip home and grab some lunch.

He looked through the rain-drizzled windscreen at the houses and yards spaced along each side of the road, the wet morning dripping off the unexceptional, overgrown, suburban landscape. He noticed the hedges and trees that needed clipping back, understanding the obvious neglect of front-yard husbandry. Who was going to go outside in this weather and take care of their garden? If it wasn't for the fact he needed the money, he too would be warm at home, lost in a book or vegged out in front of the telly. Arsenal were playing today; he'd get to see the pre-match highlights, listen to the banter of bitter ex-footballers. Loved his football did Rog!

He took a final drag on his cigarette, crushed it out, zipped up his jacket and stepped out of the car. He felt the chill of the April morning and wished it was June already. Him and the 'missus' had booked a couple of weeks in the Canary Islands. One of those all-inclusive breaks where you could eat and drink as much as you liked at no extra cost. He licked his lips at the thought of endless kebabs and bottomless sangria.

He tried to catch a glimpse of the sun but saw nothing except the watery remembrances of better days skulking behind steel colored clouds. Only a few more months and he'd be on the beach, toes in the sand, beer in hand, living the life. Despite the cold he felt an inner warmth, the glow of expectation and the tingle of excitement. He turned from the car and walked down the street, looking up at the house numbers as he went.

## Number 26, Sebastopol Terrace, Mrs. Patel - sounded a bit foreign?

She was one of the lucky individuals who would get to enjoy his company today.

His job with the insurance firm brought him into contact with all manner of people, taking him all over the city. Although everything was slowly being computerized there were still customers, especially the older folk, who preferred to pay their premiums in cash. Theirs was a monthly remittance and, although not a lot of money, worth the collection. When he calculated that he saw perhaps ten to twenty people a day, with an average payment of five pounds, the money soon added up. The *Super* had told him his was the most important job of all, that without the money there really wouldn't be a business. This made the handfuls of hot change, crumpled banknotes and promises of tomorrow all the more worthwhile.

Just one short year ago, Roger had been a retiring serviceman after spending half a lifetime in the R.A.F. He'd joined as a boy soldier, escaping from an electrician's apprenticeship in the hope of greener pastures and bluer skies. Looking back, it probably wasn't the wisest thing to have done. He blamed his older brother. Derek, who'd joined a couple of years before him, had sent postcards from places like Singapore and Hong Kong. Fantastic faraway lands, where possibilities were endless. His brother had spun tales of good times, great food, perfect beaches—and the local girls.

### Oh, those local girls! Such pretty titties!

After joining he was immediately posted to not-so-sunny Scotland, a classic case of *not* being careful what you wished for. Instead of sun-kissed palms he got wind-swept moorland.

Leaving the service had been hard. Twenty-three years of institutionalization had taken its toll. Supplied with accommodation, food, money and a secure work environment, the outside world seemed, by comparison, empty and harsh. Sure, they'd prepared him for civilian life, given him the mandatory courses, but with no safety net, no recourse and nothing but more of this, they'd finally cast him loose with even fewer guarantees. He'd quickly found work as a salesman in the newly expanding telemarketing industry selling New World wines. The idea was that you sat behind a desk and called up unsuspecting winos...

*"Hello. Is this Mrs. George?"*

*"Yes."*

*"Would you like to buy some wine?"*

*"No."*

Such was the depth of conversation Roger was participating in. Clearly the killer instinct of telephonic marketing was a branch of sales he wasn't cut out for.

Not taking rejection well, and loathing the hate emanating from silent telephones, he moved onto insurance sales, and then into collections. Of course, he could cajole a lonely pensioner into a *necessary* policy, but why would he? Bullying old people, men and women, into believing their families would be responsible for their debt was child's play. In the beginning he'd followed the company line of pursuing ever-increasing sales goals. Policy after policy was signed, sealed, and delivered – but at what cost? Profit at the price of a bad conscience; the feelings of remorse that remained with him on countless sleepless nights. The collections were much better; straightforward work that didn't require the use of subterfuge or the ability to tap into a Machiavellian mindset. He'd an honest face, so he was told. The clients trusted him, and this helped to make his job just that much easier.

He pushed open the iron gate, walked up the path, and rang the bell. The garden was neat and tidy and virtually weed free. No sign of dogs. He hated dogs, didn't like cats much either. He could hear the bell ringing deep inside the house. Eventually, after what seemed an eternity, he heard shuffling, a rustling of papers and the scrape of furniture on wooden floors. The clientele were not particularly quick but there again he wasn't exactly in a rush. Mrs. Patel opened the door.

*"Hello Roger."*

*"Morning Doris. How are you?"*

*"Oh, you know. Well as can be expected I suppose."*

Roger was dreading the conversation; he knew this polite interlude was leading to a climax he didn't want to confront – the part where he asked her for money and where she told him she had none. This would be the fifth time now and without the requisite funds he would have to strike her off.

He knew how important the life policy was to her; Mrs. Patel had a granddaughter with a young baby. Given her health issues, her age, the fact that she probably didn't have too much more of her mortal coil to shuffle, she was no doubt hoping that she could at least leave *something* for her.

*"Have you come for the money Roger?"*

He smiled, opened his heart, and then his mouth. "Oh, no," he said, "I was just in the neighborhood and thought I'd pop round to check on you." The conversation continued. Details of her granddaughter, his sons, the bin collections on Thursday, her arthritis and his tricky knee. Did he know that TESCO had raised the price of milk by sixpence?

The door closed and Roger made his way back down the path. Stopping at the gate, he pulled the ledger out of his satchel and opened it up to the *policies paid* page. Licked his pencil – strange habit – found the entry for Mrs. P. and ticked the appropriate box.

### Paid!

Reaching into his pocket he pulled out his wallet, found a five pound note and deposited it into the brown envelope with the rest of the morning's takings. That was the third old lady this week he'd anonymously subsidized. At this rate of financial extension, he was going to have to find himself another job.

The perfunctory angel made his way up the hill, got back into the car, turned on the radio, and drove away.

Mrs. P's daughter would be round that afternoon. *She'd enjoy that*, he thought.

# QUIZ NIGHT

*England 1989...*

TIRES SPLASHED THROUGH PUDDLES, water spraying the windscreen as the once pristine Ford came to a gravel opened -sliding stop. Rain beat off the roof, wipers protesting their last before the key was disengaged. A brume of heavy metal-infused cigarette smoke escaped as Trevor the door and crunched towards the pub.

The Three Cups public house — the last bastion of civilized village society. Cheap cheer and a warm fireside welcome to the recently unemployed of the local engine factory — the major employer in the area. The warming of relations between cold war antagonists meant that regiments in Germany no longer required tanks to withstand the threat of communist menace. No tanks meant no engine factory, no engine factory — no bloody work.

Trevor had looked for other work; and done a bit here and there. A spot of wall papering, gardening, fixing cars for family members; nothing of any substance. He knew there were only two options if he was ever to rejoin the ranks of the employed. Go back to school or move.

What was it the bleeding politicians had said? *"Get on your bike!"* All very well, but where the hell was he going to cycle to?

The first couple of months living on severance had been idyllic. Of course, he'd done the sensible thing, booking himself a two-week vacation to the Costa Brava. Better to be pissed off and miserable in Spain than suicidal in rain-washed Yorkshire. But the senoritas and sangria had seriously dented his resources, causing deep-seated desperation to set in. Even so, it wasn't the trip he regretted, rather the fact that it was months since he'd seen the sun.

Luckily, he'd met Linda.

Although alcohol induced, the sight of her stood at the end of the bar in her flower-print dress and cherry-gold earrings had been enough to get his motor running. Not the absolute prettiest but she was warm and considerate — the sheet-side sympathy she'd shown him on her days off more than making up for her failings. For a bigger girl she was pretty limber, the way she smelt on rain-soaked mornings, delicious. Better a couple of extra hours in bed with her than queuing with the human flotsam down at the labor exchange. There were other advantages too, besides her voluptuous bosom and her spandex encased derriere: Linda worked behind the bar at The Three Cups.

\* \* \* \*

Bill had done what he could to revive flagging village life. Since the factory closure he'd noticed the disappearance of the smiling faces propped against his bar. People were still drinking; it was just that they looked so bloody miserable while they were doing it. He'd racked his brains, pondered his failing business. How was he to rescue the pub from this creeping Titanic disaster?

To begin with he'd taken a shilling off a pint, but cheap booze only went so far. After a couple of days of euphoric disorder and a cash-filled register, enthusiasm waned. The dance on the other hand had been quite the success — the bump and grind of the Friday night disco. Its popularity probably accounted for the upsurge in perambulators one was seeing around the village these days – that and the cheap beer of course.

He'd tried talent night on Thursdays. It was nothing much to write home about, quickly turning into a couple of die-hards dominating the karaoke machine. An open mic and a willing audience always attracted the dross. Casio heaven for bedroom-bound composers, guitared mayhem from closet rock stars. Fortunately, it'd soon withered and died.

He'd quickly replaced it with live music evenings, invited bands and singers playing for semi-interested drunks. Enthusiastic amateurs filling the ears of the already depressed with the dirge of folk music. Songs about mine closure, the power of the unions, a socialist utopia brought about through cheap beer and overtime, all treated with equal disdain.

But best was quiz night: it was a hit. A full pub with full (discounted) glasses — and an animated public engaged in genuine social intercourse.

\* \* \* \*

Linda was in charge of preparing the questions, using Bill's old school textbooks that lay around the house. Twenty hard-hitting facts split over four categories: **history**, **geography**, **sport**, and **general stuff**.

The pub would sit in silent reverence while the questions were asked, coming alive as the whispered excitement of known answers and drawn blanks were mumbled into pints of bitter. The questions would be repeated with the usual admonishments from Bill.

*"No copying now. All your own work lads and lasses."*

The stakes were high. The prize was fifty pounds to the winner.

\* \* \* \*

Trevor found the questions in the bedside drawer alongside the extra batteries and the oil she liked to use — carefully typed and double spaced. That first Thursday was fantastic, the moment he'd been handed the fifty pounds electric. He'd never earned money so easily. After the first three weeks of straight wins he decided to play it cool; not everybody knew he was doing the boudoir shuffle with Linda. But in a small village, things soon get out.

With more than a hundred pound in winnings pocketed over the last couple of months, he was optimistic as he pushed open the door to the pub this Thursday night.

\* \* \* \*

*"When you're ready ladies and gents, your first question..."*

He scribbled down the memorized answer; too easy when forewarned.

Then, *"Who was...?"*

Again, his pencil coursed across the page.

After twenty questions the papers were collected and given up for marking. The juke box kicked into life. Eager customers stampeded the bar.

Once again, the microphone crackled, and Bill addressed the dearly beloved.

*"So here are the results from the German jury."* Old joke, but it always got a laugh.

*"In third... You again? Mary!"* followed by applause.

*"In second...Oliver?"* and then, *"Well done, you brainy git!"*

*"And in first place...oh, my God, Harry!"*

Trevor was furious the second his name wasn't mentioned. He'd copied the questions, learnt them by heart, practiced that afternoon in the café. He knew his answers were correct. Paris was the capital of Germany, the rain in Spain falls mainly in Milan, and Oscar Wilde was the butchest man in England!

"Fuck! It!"

He watched the lucky recipient walk to the bar to collect his winnings before disinterestedly sticking his nose back into his glass, his attention diverted from the knowing look and clasped hug Linda gave the winner. A young handsome lad from out of town with one of those things you couldn't get for love nor money ... a job. Clearly Linda had seized upon an opportunity and put her soft, round, wiles to good use.

### Any port in a storm, and something about opportunity only knocking once?

Trevor finished his pint, put down his glass and made for the door. Maybe next week he would have more luck. He'd work on his smile a bit and have a word with Linda.

# CHRISTMAS IN THE TRENCHES

*England 2011...*

I HUNKER DOWN BETWEEN THE folds of the couch, the crash of crockery and banging of pans ringing in my ears and resonating off floral-printed palisades like artillery shells falling on a Somme trench. I pray for the next twenty-four hours to pass as quickly as possible but there's little I can do to protect myself from the friendly fire of Christmas preparation. The horrors already experienced are nothing compared to the human assault which even now pounds on my front door.

I brace myself for the attack, check the batteries in the remote control—the television, my last line of defense—and try to ignore the creeping barrage. The thuds begin again, and I cringe and shake. The tremor in my left hand betrays my abject cowardice — my right eye twitches uncontrollably.

The build-up to familial battle is always a stressful time. It's not so much the fighting, it's the waiting, the not knowing, the uncertainty of a fresh campaign. We hoped it would be all over by 1914's Christmas. However, it would seem that Christmas is just the beginning.

Defensive fairy-lights have been strung, and silver streamers hang around the house like concertinaed barbed wire. Colored baubles and kid-cut snowflakes hang from everything in remembrance of soldier superstition. There is only so much I can do to escape my fate. If my rifle and bayonet can't save me then maybe a Christmas angel can. The winter barrage has been sustained for nearly a month now, the cacophony of jingling bells and chorused carols screaming their mayhem, crashing devastation through radios and television sets. Weeks of preparation have gone into what has become the annual festive campaign. Having failed to learn the lessons of holidays past, we must stupidly repeat the mistakes of Christmases long, long ago.

Outside the weather has closed in, snow hiding the shell holes in the back yard and blanketing the unkempt battlefield in a pristine mantel of white. Birds hop between bushes, foraging for red berries neglected by Mother Nature's bitter frost. There is a kinship, as, like beasts, we too are subjects of King Winter although not daring to venture into the no-man's-land of ice and snow.

Luckily, we've stocked up on provisions. It would be fair to say we have enough food in the bunker to feed an army. Family members who only days before were morose and anxious are now filled with the joy of Christmas, careless of the coming battle. Thoughts of better times and home-baked goodness fill the waiting hours detracting us from what still must be achieved. Once the whistle is blown there are no choices left and we'll be obligated to fulfill our duties. For God, King, and country we must grab ourselves by the Christmas balls and go over the top.

There they go again — the clanging chimes of doom at the front door. I look at the willing victims laid out in the bottom of the trench, sprawled in front of the television; poor innocents who know not what they are about to receive.

Eager as new recruits to prove themselves they've already dressed and are ready for the quagmire of Christmas. Donned in water stained slippers and clad in Sponge Bob and Disney pajama fatigues, they can't wait for the battle to begin.

My sergeant calls my name from the kitchen, where even now she is finalizing the finishing touches to the coming armistice feast. Enough food to feed a small African nation has been prepared and paraded for those who can drag themselves away from the horror of Christmas morning television. The Santa Claus automaton on top of the fridge starts to chime. The sharp campanology of its machine-gunned bullets whistle and shriek around me; the rattle of instant death seems close at hand.

### Why me, why now, why not them?

The sergeant bellows again and I'm forced to accept the duty placed upon me, just as I accepted the King's chocolate shilling all those Christmases ago. I reach up from the parapet, grab the wooden ladder of will and pull myself up from the couch.

### Go. Go. Go!

Clasping my can of beer in one hand I grit my teeth, emerging from the trench into the wintery wilderness. I see my objective in the distance, focus myself, and make my way towards the front door. It's no use skulking behind the furniture as the IKEA-compressed wood offers little protection. I press forward, slipping and sliding on wooden floors as my socks struggle to grip the puddled morass of my suburban Flanders fields — pushing through the branches of the Christmas tree, lumbering past the plastic snowman.

I kick in his general direction and he goes down in a fizz of sparks, a fart of expelled air.

The bell knells its diabolical dirge as the thump-thump of hand artillery smashes onto wooden panels. Why me, God? Why me? I have so much to live for! With one last superhuman effort I unbolt the latch, flick the catch, and swing open the final obstacle.

Light floods into darkened spaces. Perhaps this is it. Perhaps this is my final journey, the peace I've been waiting for — the out-of-body experience we've all tried to believe in.

### No such luck!

There they are, right on time — the enemy. Armed to the teeth with festive goodwill and store-bought cheer. Clearly their advance was successful. We stand together on this field of Elysium.

### Eye to eye, cheek to cheek, jowl to jowl.

I move in for close combat, thrusting my hand forward. The enemy counters, blocks my attack, grasping my hand in a practiced pincer grip! I try to hide the look of horror in my eyes, deceiving myself that this death will be quick and painless...

### Death by Christmas. The in-laws have arrived!

# THE BOX

*England today…*

Y OU USED TO SEE them everywhere, the post-office red of cast iron sentinels celebrating everything that was British about Britain. Embossed with monarch's cipher, one could trace the date of the telephone booth by the type of crown steel-stamped into its lintel; king's crown, queen's crown, a history lesson in metal, recalling the halcyon days of Empirical conquest.

Crimson beacons in an otherwise dour and soggy landscape, radiating the hope that was only a series of dial tones away. One could transport oneself via the magic of Mr. Bell's genius and suddenly be connected to the other side of the world. No longer the driving rain, ocean-sized puddles and biting cold – instead the balmy climes of Florida, the *joie de vivre* of *la Belle France*. A public time capsule, an individual transportation device activated by inserting lustrous silver coins and dialing launch codes. The digits were rotated and then, in anticipation of ringtone dissipation, a voice crackling through the static on the other end of the line.

"*Hello, this is Margery?*"

"*Hi Margery. This is Bill. How's the weather?*"

## **Mission accomplished, objective achieved, escapism realized.**

Crunched into ridiculously small compartments, one could escape the cares of the world by living vicariously through all too familiar voices on the end of transatlantic telephone wires. No longer were Britons trapped in sceptered isolation but were now privy to public launch platforms where the world was everybody's backyard.

A geographical extravaganza, the desired destinations were listed on the mission guide screwed to its wall. A large, mildew-stained map of the British Isles, sequestered behind plastic screening as though it were on loan from the Victoria and Albert Museum, listing each and every dial code required to accomplish the journey. The great cities of Britain, Europe and the world laid bare like ancient knowledge, just waiting to be selected and utilized by the pilot. Flight coordinates and geographical positioning for those who preferred metaphysics in easily consumed compartmentalized packages. Bite-size geography, the Grande Tour on a sixpence, who would have thunk it?

No longer limited by the boundaries of imagination or the vacuum of the pocketbook, one could now jaunt at will, exercising one's freedom to roam, ramble and wander at leisure. Satiating the wanderlust, escaping Britain's weather-induced house arrest.

Back before the war to end all wars (the first not the second), when the box was first placed, the whole village had been in attendance. Sunday finery was the requisite dress, local dignitaries parading at the appointed hour. Fine words mumbled, cameras focused, flashed and dazzled. The inaugurate call made, whilst muffled singing of "God Save the King" and "Rule Britannia" penetrated through thick glass.

The telephone box was the very model of British engineering, the door swinging open on newly oiled hinges, the bright shiny scarlet paint of the G.P.O. silken to the touch. The sheer size of the iron altar cast at the local foundry — now a supermarket — was a marvel in itself. Lit by newfangled corporate-installed electric, the bare bulb illuminating its pristine interior.

This modern invention of long-distance communication was a wonder to behold and came equipped with all the pre-requisites of 1908. There was an ashtray to hold one's cigarette, as talking and smoking just wasn't etiquette. An umbrella stand inhabited the corner and a coat hook was provided on the back of the door for raincoats and top hats. Shelves had been placed below the Bakelite telephone apparatus to contain the directory listing everybody in the market town's catchment area. The postmaster general designers had thought of everything.

The public stood aghast at the gargantuan task of recording everyone's name, address and telephone number, an achievement comparable to the building of the pyramids, the transcription of the Bible, the erection of the great Chinese wall. Marvelous what Englishmen could do when they put other nations' men to task.

Little wonder the empire spanned half the globe, and the sun never set on the Union Jack. The divine right we islanders were blessed with was helping to save the nations of the world. Spreading **Brutishness** one country at a time, so that no matter their creed or color, they could enjoy afternoon tea, cricket and imperialism (((oppression.)))

* * * *

These days the phone booth isn't quite so grand. It still serves as a monument, though now to a country in decline and depression. The empire's long gone, as are the coat hooks and umbrella stands. The windows smashed out by local hoodlums and replaced with cheap plastic, bearing the scratched names of lovers, haters and rival football supporters.

### Carved memorial in faux glass.

The paint is no longer pristine. The box probably two or three times its original size, judging by the thick layers of post-office red lathered upon it over the decades. Its interior is now dirty and smelly, the original Bakelite apparatus replaced by something stainless steeled and plastic blued. The directories have been torn out, but the map of Britain is still hidden behind the plastic. Now barely visible due to the scorch marks from fireworks ignited inside the booth.

A dense mixture of odors permeates the interior, all declaring its misuse as urinal, spittoon, meeting place for local junkies and God only knows what else. Over the decades the box has been used by bereaved parents, persistent wooers, desperate messengers, teenage lovers, rain dodgers, bus-waiters, and all manner of humanity from every location.

It has served Pakistanis, Hindustanis, Bangladeshis and Jamaicans. Greeks and Turks and even the indigenous Yorkshire population. The booth is no longer the tele-transporter of yore but instead a remembrance to the generations it has attracted through its creaking portal.

For the moment it still stands in the center of the village down by the duck pond. However, there are rustlings that it will be taken away and replaced with a shiny new plastic box. No longer owned and maintained by the G.P.O., but by some Scandinavian firm, with call-centers in Vietnam and operators with unpronounceable names.

Don't they care that this scarlet icon is all we have left of the golden age our grandparents once enjoyed? Its national importance comparable to the traditional British pub, fish and chips, the local Chinese take-away. Americans arrive in their fancy cars, take their photographs and tell us how quaint we are, how they wish America had the depth of history and culture that we enjoy. We smile back of course, and from behind bad dentistry hate them for their money and their good looks.

> ***Lose our phone box, lose our identity.***
> ***Lose our identity, lose everything.***
> ***Lose everything—lose the world.***

What then? Allow ourselves to be sucked up by the mélange of Europeanism and its insidious permeating effluence, slowly choking the highways and byways of our sovereign nation?

### *NEVER!*
### A declaration of war if ever there was one.

Championed by the local history society, we'll fight them all the way. Who do they think they are, taking away that which is rightfully ours? What next – our homes, our wives, our livelihoods? On the beaches and in the air, down by the duck pond and behind the chippy, we will resist. We've fought back Romans, Normans, Spaniards, French, Dutch, Nazis and Polish immigrants. We will not be subjected to the brutal hand of corporate attrition. Down with Big Brother and his goose-stepping iron heel.

### The box will not be moved!

Everything else is gone! *BRITISH STEEL, BRITISH RAILWAYS, BRITISH COAL, BRITISH EMPIRE* — passed over and forgotten. But the box still survives, its electric light dimly illuminating the village square.

### Maybe that's the last thing they can never take from us!

# CHOPPER JOHN

*London 1936...*

DUSK DREW IN AS rain pattered off windows, bringing an end to yet another nondescript London day. The grey fug of Piccadilly hung about the rooftops and the November cold nipped at crowds running for buses and home-cooked meals.

Bill fumbled with the door to the studio, turned the lock and ambled over to the microphone standing on his desk. He'd done it a thousand times, used his loquacious larynx to lull the young and weary to sleep with once-upon–a-times and happily-ever-after's. He sat down, placed the headphones on his head and waited for his cue.

A voice crackled in his ears, "And now over to London, to Uncle Bill Brewer and his goodnight story."

**"Cue Bill. Play music. And ... intro."**

The light above the studio door switched from green to red. He was on the air.

*"Hello children everywhere. This is Uncle Bill. I am sure that before you climb the wooden hill to Bedfordshire and wait for the sandman's magic dust to carry you off to*

*Dreamland you would love to hear a story. Would you like to hear my story?"*

All around the country children, pinched pink from hot baths, pyjammered and nightgowned, sat before radiograms in anticipation of tonight's tale. The ritual of rushed teeth cleanings and hurried suppers ensured prime spots in front of crackling speakers.

*"Tonight's story is about Chopper John, a woodsman who lives and works in the ten-acre wood. His days are filled with the sounds of the forest and the little birds and animals that live beneath its spreading canopy. Are you ready?"*

Screamed confirmation from a thousand small voices echoed throughout Radio Land.

Bill had been in radio since it was silent. What he didn't know about broadcasting would fit on the back of a postage stamp. He'd done it all, seen it all, and met everybody who was anybody. His career spanned thirty years and Broadcasting House was more a home than it was a place of work. Bill was loved by the children of Britain both young and old.; his chocolate tinted annunciation a confection to their eager ears.

*"Every morning Chopper John would get out of bed, yawn loudly, put on his favorite red shirt and eat his breakfast in the kitchen. Toast and marmalade with two boiled eggs."*

Bill reached into the cupboard below the desk and pulled out the bottle — medicinal of course, for celebration purposes only. He screwed off the cap and poured a finger or six into the white enameled cup in front of him.

*"Then he would pick up his axe and head into the forest."*

Bill put the cup to his mouth and gulped its contents. He'd often been asked the secret of his success, how he managed to cultivate the rich warm tobacco tones for which he was known and adored.

*"Chopper John walked into the wood, whistling as he went, passing all the friendly woodland creatures on his way. Rabbits and squirrels lined the path waiting for Chopper John just as they did each morning."*

Children sat in awe, the tale of Chopper John filling their sleepy little minds with images of fun, furry, creatures scampering through bushes. Happy days and even happier dreams lay ahead.

*"Because it was such a beautiful day, Chopper John decided to ignore the whisperings of the creatures. Their acerbic, back-stabbing remarks, meant to hurt a man who had given his all for the corporation – a man who'd laid down his life for radio."*

The chipped cup hit the top of the desk again. Uncle Bill fought the grimace on his face as the bite of alcohol stung his throat.

*"The sun warmed his body and the breeze blew through his golden hair. The insidious comments made by the newly installed management team would not deter him. Vicious mean bastards trying to get rid of Uncle Bill and replace him with some snot-nosed wanker with no experience."*

Children turned to parents with bright wholesome smiles, the sound of leafy woodlands dancing in their ears. Parents put down newspapers and knitting needles and turned up the volume on the radiogram.

*"Chopper John was not a bitter man but if he had been, he would've shoved their gold watch so far up their*

arse that they'd have to open their mouths to check the time… as he wandered into the clearing."

A bald man rushed into the control room and slashed a finger across his throat. Uncle Bill ignored him and refilled the cup.

"As he meandered through cool, leafy glades, Chopper John decided that he should tell the truth, and let his young listeners know what bastards the directors really were. Money-grabbing, scum-sucking boy-lovers, who wouldn't know the meaning of a hard day's work if it jumped up and kicked them in the balls … and took his hunting rifle off his back."

Children sat half dozing, half dreaming as they lived the story floating through the speakers. Fathers removed pipes from mouths and mothers hastily bookmarked pages.

Now there was a crowd of people in dark suits inside the control room —banging on the glass, gesticulating wildly and mouthing mute threats. Bill smiled, reached into his pocket, and brought out the revolver.

"Chopper John loved to hunt, and a plump pheasant would make him a lovely supper. Pheasant in rich gravy with potatoes and carrots, and the bastards will rue the day they got rid of Uncle Bill. Arse-licking sycophants with nothing in their empty heads but shit and sawdust."

The pistol exploded and clattered to the floor, smoke curling around Bill's slumped body as security guards kicked their way through splintered wood.

\* \* \* \*

The bald-headed producer pressed the transmit button on his microphone.

"Unfortunately, the story of Chopper John will have to wait for another time, and so we wish our listeners sweet dreams and happy thoughts. Goodnight from Chopper John and goodnight from Uncle Bill."

Parents stared at each other. That hadn't sounded like Uncle Bill.

Very strange!

Radiograms around the country were turned off as sleepy children were carried to bed.

**Goodbye Chopper John. Goodbye Uncle Bill.**

# THE UNKNOWN SOLDIER

*Deepest, darkest Yorkshire, England, 1977…*

THE ROOM WAS DARK and shadowed, the curtains open. Heavily laden battle-ship clouds drifted overhead. Rain ran down the windows. The garden was a morass but judging by the activity at the pond, the ducks were making hay. Large ripples ellipsed and expanded — watery rings around reed-ridden banks.

"Weather for ducks," was what his grandfather said whenever it rained. Another of his gems was, "Where there's muck there's brass," conjuring up images of highway-robbed bullion lying forgotten in roadside ditches, waiting to be dug up, rinsed off, and spent on lollipops and lead soldiers.

Harry loved to visit his grandparents; loved the mystery the old, damp, creaking house possessed. The sitting room was filled with the treasures of ages — the piano in the corner of the room that nobody played, the two shiny brass artillery shells standing guard by the fireplace, the large framed photograph on the mantelpiece. The sepia-colored man in the picture dressed as a soldier, spit and polished, holding an ancient rifle — a forgotten protagonist of a long-forgotten war.

A fire roared in the hearth. Because of the rain, the chimney didn't draw quite as well as it should, the backlash of smoke giving an earthy scent and a haze to an already darkened room. He was in the back parlor, as his nan called it; a living room in modern day parlance. Obviously if there was a back parlor, then there had to be a front parlor. That was the room he wasn't allowed to play in.

The mysteries of the front parlor had only been revealed to him on a couple of occasions. Once, when his grandfather had run out of pipe tobacco and he'd followed him into the room, the other when his nan had been distracted whilst dusting and using the Hoover on the deep-piled carpet. On both occasions he'd caught fleeting glances of the room's interior before being shooed away.

The front parlor was special. Or rather, the front parlor was for special people.

Unlike the sitting room, the front parlor was lightly papered with a floral print. There was a large picture window at the end allowing sunlight to enter on warm Yorkshire days. From memory he recalled a mirrored cabinet that bounced the sun around the room, creating a sense of well-being, pulling at the corners of mouths, inducing smiles. Upon entering the room on a day like today, it was as though a great weight was lifted from one's shoulders — the lubrication required to oil the spring in one's step. His nan had told him she stored her best crockery in there, that and her Belgium lace. They were never used of course, but that's where they were stored, just in case. Good to know, he thought, just in case!

You could see the ever-shut door to the front parlor when entering the house via the kitchen. Through the kitchen door and into the hallway where the paraphernalia necessary to combat the harshness of inclement British weather stood.

Next to the umbrella stand and beneath the coats was a large ceramic elephant's foot his grandfather had inherited from the big house on the hill when the lady had died. Apparently, he'd done a bit of gardening for her, her eternal thanks expressed in Wedgewood gigantism.

A perennial biscuit tin sat on the table, though it'd been years since there'd been any biscuits inside. The tin was red with a picture of a lady wearing a crown waving from a horse-drawn carriage. Around the tin were images of places in London titled variously as 'The Tower' or 'Big Ben.' The tin was full of old coins. Some brass, some silver, and some gold in color. The coins had barely pronounceable names, such as 'thrupenny-bits,' 'sixpences', 'farthings,' and 'half-crowns.' There was even a gold sovereign, but his nan kept that in the front parlor in the glass cabinet for the special people who never visited.

The fire blazed, the logs spat. Wooden shrapnel flew from the fireplace and bounced off the fire guard. Harry's granddad had told him the wood was wet, that the fire would dry it out. Made sense, if you thought about it.

\* \* \* \*

Once again Harry looked upwards at the large black-and-white photograph on the mantel and wondered who it was. There was a familiarity in the stance, the nose, the ears, and yet he couldn't put his finger on it. Clearly the young man was very brave, dashing in his soldier's uniform — flat campaign cap on his head, puttees wrapped around his legs, rifle slung over his khaki-clad shoulder. He looked like one of the characters from the old movie reel pictures they showed at the Odeon Picture House before the main flick on Saturday mornings.

The clock above the mantel struck the hour, the pendulum weights slipping on the chains. His grandfather walked into the room.

"Time for a cuppa," he said, shuffling toward his chair, paper under his arm, teacup in hand. There was something familiar in the features of his grandfather that he hadn't noticed before. Harry watched him as he slipped into the big comfy chair, slurped his tea, flicked open his newspaper and started to read. They sat in amicable silence, each enjoying the company of the other.

Harry looked out the window, watched as the rain slid down the glass and thought that his granddad was right.

This really was "weather for ducks."

# TERRACE-ORISM

*England, Saturday afternoon...*

AN IMPASSIONED, DISEMBODIED VOICE screams from stadium speakers, *"There's only the goalie to beat. He's passed the midfielders, out-maneuvered the last defender, charging like a bull towards the ten-yard line."*

The goalie, anticipating the rush of danger, moves out of the goal mouth — the last line of defense in a team with more holes than a dolphin-safe fishing net. With steely-eyed determination he sallies forth, the spark of self-delusion shining brightly — hope of a last minute away-day victory.

The striker's world is filled with the shape shifting blues and whites behind the net; the goalie's gloved hands as big as salvers. The last chance to score before the whistle blows, the difference between glory and defeat.

*In the stands the corrugated metal roofing creaks and groans in the midday sun. Shafts of light lance down on the spectators below, striking the gathered legions through burst rivets and rusted seams. A sea of blood red and bruised blue awash with September sunshine.*

*The home derby — a day begun with good intent, that will inevitably end in blood, tears, and incarceration down at the local nick. Despite the pretense of sportsmanship and camaraderie at the biannual confrontation between local rivals, the outcome is always the same. The hate generated by twenty-two miles of separation simmers and stews until match day boils it over. No quarter is expected, and none will be given.*

The speakers trumpet their litany of commentated mayhem. **"He only has the goalkeeper to beat. Can anybody stop this man?"**

With slow mechanical machinations the keeper plods his way through mud and sod, his arms spread wide, blocking the field of view, narrowing the angle of shot. This is the only moment that will count, the only moment remembered. Everything else forgotten and for nothing should the striker achieve his aim. He can't let it happen. Defeat at the hands of their fiercest rivals is not an option. With one last supreme effort, with seconds ticking on the clock, he digs in his studs and rushes forward.

*The red scarves, having scaled the barrier fence, fight their way forward through closed blue ranks. Fights have already broken out and the roof-raising chants are now drowned by the shouts of men committed to battle. Bottles smash as spit-soaked bobbies react to whistles and departmental commands. A thin line of monochromatic authority adrift in an ocean of color, they attempt to separate the warring factions. Half-filled plastic cups and empty bottles take Agincourt flight, the debris darkening and descending from sun-striped skies.*

As the striker draws back his foot in readiness to bury the ball in the netting of his opponent's goal, the keeper spreads across his horizon. The striker senses his moment. Ninety minutes of pure adrenalin encapsulated in one final shot.

Heart thumps, lungs rasp, and muscles tense. Power surges through sinew as he spears the ball towards the goal.

*Already the coppers are in trouble. Police helmets are on the ground and personal revenge is exacted by an anonymous crowd. Men stand toe to toe, murderous intent on their faces, as they rain blow after blow in a vicious exchange of boots and fists.*

### *"Take that you twat! Fuck off back to where you came from you West Yorkshire prick!"*

*Combatants clash in a sea of arms and legs, a river of blood and tissue, a cacophony of shouts and screams. Trapped between the plastic chairs, a man goes down in a flurry of limbs and curses. Another leaps headlong into the crowd from one of the steel stanchions. Pain and mayhem reign in what will be recorded in tomorrow's papers as the worst home derby for years.*

The boot strikes the ball and the black-and-white projectile sails through the air. Water and grass crease from its surface, the impact of leather against leather forcing it to sail and curve through the air. The striker feels it in his core, knows that this is the final shot of the match — prays that this one will count.

The goalie leaps into the air with legs like springs, powering himself away from the ground, defying gravity and reaching for the heavens. His lightning lightening run from the goal line bringing him into position.

*The public address system goes quiet and for a brief second, antagonists hold punches in midair as they watch the drama unfold on the field below. Men momentarily forget to hate – blood runs freely down police uniforms. The crowd holds its breath.*

The Tannoy screams back to life. *"Goal!!!"*

The goalkeeper thumps hard onto wet grass, knowing he's failed, the scream of the crowd telling him what he already suspected. He had felt the ball brush his fingertips, hoped his efforts had been enough.

The striker — eyes wide, mouth open — turns on one foot, the cheer already rising in his throat. Rips off his shirt and heads for his moment of glory on the sideline. Three-two with nothing left to play for. The referee's whistle clarions time across the field; players embrace whilst others drop their shoulders and stare at the ball wedged in the back of the net.

*In the stands, cheers die on the lips of rough men intent on doing harm; combat now justified by the finality of a loss at home. They may have lost the match, but the battle on the terraces is still theirs for the winning.*

# PSEUDO SOPRANO

*Once upon a time. In America...*

THE CUSHIONS MOLDED AROUND him as Jake grabbed his beer and in a practiced one easy practiced movement sank into the couch. Another day another dollar. Hopefully tomorrow would be the same. The handyman business had really taken off. After three years of hard graft he'd managed to establish a reliable and lucrative clientele. It was peanuts by giant corporation standards – just Jake, his truck, and his fifteen-year-old son, who occasionally accompanied him on weekends.

His business was super low-tech, making for quick decisions and easy money. Living on a side of town where retirees outnumbered the working stiffs meant there was a bundle to be made. He enjoyed his job. Every day was different.

He'd seen it all from the good, to the bad, to the extremely ugly. That was the beauty of being a handyman; you got to become a professional sneak. Poking around people's homes, checking out their pictures, record collections and anything else they chose to leave out. Decorum and modesty were anathema to most of the paying public. He'd come across the most personal of items lying around bedrooms and bathrooms. From the innocuous vaginal dryness creams and male-enhancement pills to the very latest in electronic gadgetry and vacuum pleasuring devices. He'd even had the dubious honor pleasure of making the acquaintance of several personal inflatable companions. Nothing surprised him anymore.

It didn't matter. Money was money.

The truck was unloaded and garaged, the soiled rags from the day's labors tumbling in the washing machine in preparation for tomorrow. It was time for a little relaxation, some well-deserved Jake-time. He flicked a switch on the remote and the DVD sprang into life.

He was watching the latest selection from HBO, some mob series about a family in New Jersey. Good stuff. Lots of tits and stiffs, just the way he liked it. He'd spent hours living vicariously as a mobster, to the extent his ever later bedtimes were causing issues. Getting out of bed was increasingly problematic. Something had to give and usually it was the alarm clock. A quick bitch-slap and the screaming demon could be silenced at least for another five precious minutes.

He'd utilized every excuse under the sun to explain away his tardiness to his customers, telling tall tales of errant children, sick daughters, punctured tires and trucks that failed to start. Each time they'd displayed the same faux sympathy, reassuring him that it really didn't matter, that they hoped all would be well, that they were just glad to see him.

### Better late than never?

They loved Jake, he'd been doing their houses forever, had strongly recommended his services to their neighbors. He always smiled gratefully, accepted their absolution contrition, picked up his toolbox and went about his business.

The mobster series was fantastic — well filmed, well written and totally believable. The lead character was a bastard, but a lovable bastard. He exuded a level of psychopathic empathy that made him more approachable than your average mob boss. Of course, he had to enforce his territory, make sure his goons were performing to his satisfaction when dealing out the necessary violence. But wasn't it the same for any management position? The position of Godfather clearly demanded respect, and to be honest, Jake thought the hours and benefits didn't look so bad. Especially when compared to other career choices he could think of.

The large screen TV burned images into his brain, the subliminal message of violence and extortion laid down for subconscious posterity, thousands of neuron connections created with every episode he watched. Frequently, especially after a three-client day, he would catch himself dozing off halfway through the show. His mind would switch from the pseudo-reality of the living room to the manifest depths of dreams where wildest fantasies were played out in surreal brilliance.

He himself crammed 9mm shells into chrome plated pistols, beat delinquent debtors, strangled made men and generally pursued the life, liberty, and happiness of the average gangster. The dreams were so real he would wake up at night in cold sweats, the covers in disarray, staring around the room to see if he was being watched or followed. Of course, he wasn't, so drifted off to sleep again only to encounter, once more, the darker side of the New Jersey population.

One particular episode involved the mob boss shaking down an Indian restaurant. There he sat, suited and booted surrounded by hundred-dollar bills and multi-limbed goddesses, serenaded by sitar music, whilst digging into a plate of chicken vindaloo. Indian food at the very least is extremely potent and vindaloo is right up there with the madras and military-grade explosives.

**Warning: this curry will turn your innards to lava, causing you to spend the rest of tomorrow in bathroom isolation.**

Of course, that's what happened. The boss fell afoul of Delhi belly and for the rest of the episode Jake watched him race from bed to bathroom, puking and farting simultaneously with no control of his bodily functions, leaving lots of trace evidence for the Feds.

**Gandhi had truly had his revenge!**

\* \* \* \*

Jake felt his pain. He too had succumbed to delicious aromas emanating from a curry-house back in the mists of youth and had paid dearly. Like the mob boss, his enthusiastic indulgence had been his undoing. He recalled his own Olympic sprint to the bathroom, the last sheet of paper as it peeled off the roll, a story he'd told many times. He'd run to a disabled-invalid-bathroom, knowing they were always empty, and proceeded to devastate the porcelain. He'd emerged shaken, half the man he'd been, only to find a row of desperate wheelchair-bound amputees lined up in the corridor door waiting to use the convenience. Guilty as he was, the least he could do was tell them not to go inside. However, his advice had fallen on deaf ears.

\* \* \* \*

After kicking off his shorts, rubbing his nuts, and sinking into the welcome embrace of the couch, he awaited the administrations of his long-suffering wife who brought across the meal she'd prepared for his dinner. Truly a feast for the immortals – ambrosia in the form of chili con carne and bottled beer. The chili couldn't be spicy enough. He prided himself on his cool demeanor when friends would cough and splutter at the mere mention of jalapeno or break sweat at the allusion to chili powder.

**If you can choke it down when those around you are losing their cool, then you will be a curry-eater, my son. *Pussies!***

Chili was a man's meal. It wasn't just food, it was a test, a badge of honor. Hadn't one of the tasks of Hercules been to consume the entire chili reserves in the Augean stables? Or was he confusing that with an episode of *Ultimate Somethings* on one of the so-called learning channels? Either way he was prepared. He felt the heat hit the back of his throat and burn all the way down to his belly like bomber-dropped napalm.

Raising the beer to his lips, he drank greedily, emptying half the bottle in one swig. This was really living. His senses burned with the hot chili infusion, sweat watering his thinning scalp hair. Jake looked at the TV mob boss; the mob boss looked back at Jake. They were one and the same. It was hard to make out who was living vicariously, and just who through whom.

Jake, in his mind, was a *made man*. He'd started to develop an Italian east coast accent, practicing to himself every morning in the mirror. His lip would curl, his hands gesticulate wildly, his stance adjust to support his aggressive attitude.

The mobster in the mirror would stare back at Jake, repeat the expletives whilst tossing his greased hair and staring at the balding man in the saggy underwear with the protruding belly before him.

Jake liked the way he looked and had taken to wearing dark pin-striped suits when he took the 'missus' out for dinner at the local Spaghetti Warehouse. Lacking only the Trilby, the burp-gun, the gangster's mole and the black sedan, Jake personified danger.

* * * *

Day followed night and Jake was back on the job. He parked his truck outside the client's house and checked the rear-view mirror for any sign of the Feds. Nothing! Either he'd lost his imaginary tail at the coffee house or he was just too smart to be caught. They were no match for his criminal genius.

He jumped out, walked to the door and rang the bell. A dog barked somewhere inside. After a couple of seconds, the door opened.

Before him stood a woman in her early fifties—divorcee, widow, he couldn't tell but he knew that she lived alone. She smiled and they talked small. No matter the topic of conversation Jake couldn't take his focus off the lone, errant whisker poking from her chin; a survivor of the daily plucking her body no doubt endured. Something to do with higher testosterone as estrogen leaked out of them during menopause. Memories of Aunt Mary flashed through his mind, the only woman he knew with a permanent five o'clock shadow.

Chewbacca told Jake she'd have to leave but would return shortly. The over-pampered mutt, humping the kitchen stool, had to be taken to the groomer.

The conversation ended and he turned to go. As the door shut, he felt the first thrust of his bowels, quickly followed by a tsunami of heat rushing through his body. Jake farted, recognizing instantly the essence of chili. Recovering himself, he thought no more about it and went about his work. The gas persisted but Jake fought back his body's natural reaction to defecate. Wave after flaming wave of gut-wrenching spasms flashed through his lower abdomen.

The garage door opened, and the woman reversed her car out of the drive. The bumper stickers on her car declared her devotion to the cross, marking her as one of God's chosen. She waved at Jake. Jake waved back.

As the car disappeared from view, Jake knew he wasn't going to be able to maintain the status quo with the necessity brewing in his gut. What the hell was he going to do? He couldn't go in the house when she wasn't there. The last thing he needed was to be accused of breaking and entering. How does a man explain himself to a woman who comes home to find a handy-man, a window-cleaner grunting and groaning in the bathroom with his pants around his ankles?

He extinguished the fantasy and thought fast. Action was required. His mind raced and his palms sweated as he fought the desire to shit. But it had to happen, and it had to happen now.

What if she came home? There was no time to waste, the metal was hot, the iron about to strike — the turtle was rearing its ugly head.

### *Stop, drop and dump!*

He fumbled with his belt, ripped down his pants, rending the zipper useless as he did so. He braced himself against the French doors, between the air-conditioning unit and the American flag sticking out of the planter pot. Jake stared fixedly in front of him, straight into the kitchen window of a neighbor's house. Too late. No time for modesty. What would be would be. It was coming fast.

Jake let rip. Like a steaming train emerging from the mouth of a tunnel with whistle blowing, out it came. Fireworks exploded, choirs sang, and the light of heaven beamed down on the sinner. The pyroclastic flow of released gasses burned his arse cheeks, singeing his hair. He felt the hot blast shoot past his balls, splattering against the side of the Christian lady's residence.

Curiosity overcame him and he turned to view the destruction he'd wrought. The steaming pile spoke volumes as it oozed and shimmered in its own heat haze. He thought he detected the face of Jesus but quickly dismissed the idea, blaming it on the momentary stress of the situation.

He reached into his pocket, fumbled for a rag and proceeded to drag it across his arse. No time for niceties, no checking to see if he was clean. The wipe was as perfunctory as it was swift.

He discarded the rag in the grass and fought to recover himself. Looking straight ahead, he imagined he saw a shadow at the kitchen window of the house opposite but tried to dismiss the thought as rationally as possible. Speed was of the essence, the difference between discovery and escape.

Today fortune was on Jake's side. The guardian angel hovering around his nether regions had saved him in his moment of need. He invoked the spirit and gave thanks.

He heard the car coming up the drive, the slam of the door, the sound of footsteps, and panicked. He was dressed but disheveled; the evidence of his deed plain to see. He thought quickly, his mobster reactions racing for a solution.

He grabbed for the hose pipe by the side of the house. His fingers came alive, dexterously operating the faucet, directing the ensuing jet at the evidence.

Like a mobster pumping round after round from a Thompson machine gun, he obliterated the crime scene, spreading DNA far and wide.

The Christian lady popped her head around the door.

"Everything okay?"

Jake looked up, smiled and with an open-handed, Mediterranean gesture, dropped his lip, and rolled his shoulders, indicating there was no problem. The evidence was gone, the deed hidden. There was, however, still the matter of the witness at the neighboring house who had to be taken care of. Jake's imagination went into hyper-drive as he envisioned shallow graves on moonless nights.

What was he thinking?

What he really needed was an early night and some decent sleep — maybe a couple of beers and a few hours in front of the television.

It was going to be a late night.

# WARHORSE

*A bus stop in London, 1980...*

IT'S STARTING TO RAIN when I sit myself next to a man at a bus stop. Don't say much; don't have to. You know the type — late to middling in years, neatly dressed, tied and shirted, exuding a martial air. His jacket brushed, his tie shaped, his trousers creased, burnished black brogues mirrored to a shave-yourself sheen. It's always a giveaway. On his hands the faded blues and blacks of inks indelible, smudged over gnarled flesh. Tattooed beauties picked out in some foreign port and needled for posterity on willing flesh. An age when there wasn't a tomorrow, when one lived for the hour, for the possibility.

The shelter's cold and damp, stinks of piss and as per usual the bus is late. The gent next to me looks to the front, his thousand-yard stare burning holes in the concrete of the municipal Ministry-of-What-Not across the street.

Obviously, he's post ticketed for the fast-track experience – voyaged an ocean of pain, ridden the bullet train to hell, and is in no hurry to go back. Been there, done that, and purchased the rights to a t-shirt printing press of the mind. No doubt remembering when minutes lasted hours, seconds a lifetime. A time when waiting for public transport would have been a luxury, a urine-splashed bus shelter a godsend.

You can always tell. It doesn't take badges and medals, nor regimental bands and battle honors. The horror of conflict under jungle canopies and death-raked beaches... does something to a man. Marks him forever, stamps him as an initiate forged in an era of getting things done. No complaining, stiff upper lip, "*mind your p's and q's,*" back home for tea and crumpets — or more likely a beer and a cuddle at the Pig and Whistle.

Squared shoulders, straight-limbed bravado, a warrior spirit concealed within the trenches of wrinkled skin. Hard to shake memories of when the air sang.

### Dream-filled insomnia of death and destruction, oceans of sand and mud, men screaming for their mothers.

Seas of unforgotten faces left and lost on unpronounceable battlefields, on foreign shores in countries now packaged for summer holidays. The rows of white stones, part of the attraction, the Dunkirk Kodak moment to show to friends and smear onto social networks.

When thoughts of tomorrow were as improbable as moonshots, their only possession the here and now. Love today because who knew what the dawn would bring.

The rain comes down harder, pelting the shelter, water streaking down the glass, framing the tardiness of a red number seven as it splashes its way to a hurried stop. The clang of bells and the crump of pneumatics as the doors close. The old boy in front of me fishes for plastic tokens and a faded photo pass, the ephemera of a grateful nation. Life and limb given for half-price transportation but even then, only outside of rush hours and excluding Easter and Christmas. There's no complaining, no whining, just smiles as he thanks the driver and takes his seat.

Surrounded by forgetful ignorance, a public more interested in commercialism than recent history, there are no handshakes, shoulder slaps or words of gratitude. Deep down he probably likes it that way; insulated anonymity.

The bus stops and I make my way to the exit, electing to eject myself from the womb'ed warmth into the dank wet of the city. I catch his eye and he finally notices me. I voice my recognition, implore my understanding, open my mind to telepathic transmissions and broadcast my affinity with the warrior code — what it is to be a soldier.

The old boy simply looks through me. Does he recognize one of his old mates in my face or is he even now crouched in a shell hole screaming for his life, pissing himself in abject fear?

Outside, I stare up at the rain-spattered windows, the condensed fug of opaque passengers as the bus drives away. I pull my jacket around my ears, tighten my scarf, and try to avoid the puddles. The weather is really starting to close in, and I have a hungry wife and a couple of starving kids at home.

Decisions, decisions. What will it be? Chicken chow mein or egg fried rice?

# FEMME FATALE

*London city suburbs, 1980...*

THE CLOUD OF HAIRSPRAY mingled with the residual steam from the shower, condensing on the bathroom cabinet — the specter of passion-red lips barely perceptible through hand-smeared glass. An aroma of expensive soap and perfume hung in the air, energizing the senses, promising an evening of as yet unrequited pleasure. The bedroom was lit with candles, incense, and possibility. Although crumpled, the bed served adequately to showcase the little black dress, seamed sheer stockings, six-inch heels and silver necklace. Everything laid out perfectly in preparation of the evening to come.

Mirrors had been flirted with, a fashion show of dresses and skirts paraded in front of its unforgiving eye. Backwards glances cast to judge figure-hugging enhancing lingerie whilst long lacquered nails fumbled with leather straps and dithered over ridiculously small jewelry clasps. Finally, a decision was made, not that decisions couldn't be altered and prerogative exercised! After the requisite amount of indecision over neckline and hem, there was just time enough for the necessary preening. The act before the act, the scene setting and chorus of a dance hall

The dance had been announced weeks before. A new club advertised in bold text and garish colors was opening up in the high street. There hadn't been a dance club since the Roxy burned down back in '76. Promises of chandeliered excellence and champagne decadence excited local imaginations. Finally, somewhere to exercise permissive social intercourse, a place to showcase one's inner celebrity.

The invitation had been accepted, the date finalized. After a week of furtive telephone conversations and car-parked rendezvous, the decision to go was hammered out and carved in stone.

Such an evening would be an auspicious occasion at the end of any working week. However, on this particular week, a scarlet-lettered day indeed.

Plucked, preened, shaved and quaffed, a flower of womanhood stared back from the looking glass. Dark, charcoaled eyes and rouged cheeks simpered from behind caged lashes. Still glowing from the warmth of the shower, the kiss of silk stockings against freshly shaved legs was electric. The rustle of the dress as it draped over designer-store panties, the cotton hem brushing naked thighs. A Friday Night Princess in all but name, but a Friday night princess just the same.

Above the sound of the record player, the doorbell voiced its impatient demand. A flick of the curtain revealed a shadowy figure outside the front door, smoke rising from orange embers. The lights from the still running car reflected in the puddled street, the exhaust gasses misting the road.

**It was time.**

A week's worth of trepidation had expired; the moment was here; the moment was now. Turning back one last time to view his sleek silhouette in the mirror he smiled, satisfied.

*This was going to be a night to remember...*

# NASTY

*An apartment building, London, 2011...*

ZIPPING UP HIS TROUSERS, John reached over to wipe the sticky mess from his fingers. He was a three-a-day man and considering it was only ten o'clock in the morning he'd already beaten his personal best. Nothing like a bit of lesbian porn to get the motor running! Finished with the tissue, he screwed it into a ball and threw it with practiced precision into the wastepaper basket by the television, already overflowing with the lost lives of millions.

He searched under the stained cushions for the remote control and pressed *pause* — preserving his moment of ecstasy forever, the girl in the nurse's uniform frozen in mid-stroke. He shivered and reached for the discarded t-shirt. It was getting cold in the mornings.

Rolling off the couch, he landed on the detritus of a week's worth of curry containers, empty beer bottles and the accumulated collection of personal DNA worthy of Guinness Book recognition.

Scratching his arse and farting, he shoved his feet into the slippers, his yellow nails accenting the blue of the terry toweling and shuffled his way into the kitchen. Starving to death as he was, having eaten nothing since the previous evening, he was keen to discover what the cornucopia-of-crap had to offer.

Standing in front of the open refrigerator, the soft electric light broke over his matted hair, shadowing his copious folds. Like an impressionist painting of the Tuscan hills, he was for the briefest of moments a joy to behold. The Etruscan scene was broken by the loud rasping sound of flatulence curling around his arse cheeks as it made a break for freedom. Sniffing at what passed for personality, his scum-covered lips curled in a hideous smile, recognizing the aroma of curries past. Loved his chilies did John, however they didn't reciprocate. But nothing could deter him from reinitiating the cycle every time he passed the curry-house down the high street.

### "Vindaloo as hot as you can make it, and don't spare the bloody poppadoms!"

They knew him well in the restaurant. Ever since he'd taken the job down at the local shopping center, he'd become a regular figure. His persistent orders of the same arse-burning shite meant they'd quickly gotten to know him.

### "How are you today sir? Did you have a busy day sir? See you tomorrow sir. Merry Christmas sir!"

His bleary eyes stared into the cavern that was the fridge, the mold on the inside accentuating its grotto-like qualities. Miniature stalagmites hung from the now opaque glass shelves while the cure for cancer secreted itself behind an overgrown yogurt pot. Like the Holy Grail, the tin foil containers with the remnants of last night's feast offered sweet salvation. shimmered in their own heat haze.

**Let the feast begin.**
**Nothing like leftover curry.**

Before he could complete his quest, he felt the familiar churning in his belly and slammed the door quickly. Kicking over half-filled beer bottles and stampeding over crushed pizza boxes he ran, or rather waddled, as fast as he could to the bathroom. He barely had time to rip down his already christened underpants before the volcanic blast breached and splattered the pan. With a great sigh of relief, he sat in reverence, enjoying the peace that sweet release brought him.

His office, as he liked to call it, was strewn with magazines and empty cardboard toilet rolls, the floor barely visible beneath. The girlie magazines on the floor were damp from where he'd splashed.

Never having lived with a woman, standing to piss was a matter of habit rather than choice. Lurking over the pot, loosely aiming in the general direction of the empty toilet freshener, he managed to get most of it in, most of the time. The toilet brush, still pristine in its shop-bought plastic, stood like a monument to forgotten hygiene.

What did it matter? It was just him!

Dragging the paper across his hairy arse, he inspected it briefly before discarding it and reaching for the next sheet. Like an automaton he repeated the process until he was nearly clean. Good shade this morning, obviously the curry house had upped their game! John enjoyed a challenge and clearly the curry chef at the Taj Mahal enjoyed his work.

He flushed and turned to watch the cyclone of crap disappear down the bend. Sniffing his fingers and scratching his nuts, he pulled up his pants. He caught sight of his watch and cursed. He was going to be late to work if he didn't get his backside in gear. He shouldn't have committed to that last five-fingered- shuffle. Now he was going to be late. He'd been warned twice already! Never mind the shower, that would have to wait until tonight, as would the toothpaste and the hairbrush. There was no time.

Walking over to the table where he'd left his work clothes from the previous evening, he began to dress. Luckily the uniform they'd provided for him was nice and warm. Given the horrible, grey December day, he was going to need it. It wasn't too bad, and to be honest it was as though it had been tailored for him. The large, red jacket fit him perfectly as did the huge blousy trousers. It was just the black boots he hated — they bit into his bunions and made his feet sweat.

He ran for the door, stopped, remembered, and returned to the table.

### Fuck!

He'd nearly forgotten the white beard! The manager would burst a blood vessel.

### What was Santa Claus without his beard?

# THE JAVELIN CATCHER'S APPRENTICE

*A travelling circus in England, 1880s...*

FOUR YEARS HAD PASSED since willing boys with bright eyes and quick minds had apprenticed themselves into the ancient art of javelin catching. Fleet of foot and deft of hand, six eager prospects had started out on the road to enlightenment. That was a lifetime ago. Now there was just Jack. Devotion, application and self-sacrifice had helped him through the arduous training.

"It isn't for everybody," old Johan had told him. "If it was easy, then anybody could do it."

Johan's looks defied his sixty years, his athletic body lending grace to his aged frame. The scar tissue of javelins past scarred his skin. He was a Teutonic athlete, a consummate showman — master of airborne dexterity.

\* \* \* \*

Stilted men in garish costumes waded through massed humanity.

"*Roll up, roll up! Get your tickets 'ere! Bearded ladies, tigers from Bengal, strange two-headed beasties from*

*Kathmandu. Prepare your mind for what your eyes will never believe! Get your tickets or forever remain in shadowed ignorance. Step forward, ladies and gentlemen, enter the tent of knowledge – illumination awaits you."*

Men and women thronged to the red and white striping of the big-top, encapsulating their away-day excitement, focusing their wide-eyed amazement. Greedy hands clutched toffee apples and brazier-roasted nuts. The aroma of baked pies and pastries mingled with the scent of elephant dung and soiled straw. A heady, hypnotic brew of aromatic curiosity.

The crowd was filled with top-hatted, whiskered gentlemen in Sunday suits, bustled and rouged bonneted ladies, dragging sailor-suited children into the darkness of the tent. Herded and cajoled, penny-pinched and harangued, the holiday ripple was pierced with the laughs and cries of excited expectation — the shrill voices of mothers pursuing errant children. As they passed from the shadows into the light there was an audible gasp, the expanse of the big-top spreading before them. Candy-striped poles and bright shining mirrors — an arena of expectation where the gladiators of entertainment would perform (including appreciative public.)

\* \* \* \*

The act was simple enough. However, the courage and tenacity of the performer was what wooed the crowd. Burlesqued acrobats would climb the ropes of the grand-trapeze where they would hurl silver-steeled, rainbow-fletched javelins down into the arena.

Beautiful, nubile young women and muscular young men would hang in the rigging like vengeful Valkyries, hurling rod after silver rod at their target below.

Johan, with the grace and speed of a dancer and the experience garnered through years of performance, would fling himself from side to side, avoiding the deadly shafts, grabbing them out of the air with calculated ease. Then with eye-defying dexterity and an exaggerated flourish, he would hurl them at the straw bull's-eye-painted targets positioned around the ring. The continuous *thunk-thunk* as the shafts whistled through his hands and struck their targets. A true master of his craft and a confirmed crowd pleaser; his devotion to his craft, plain for all to see. The continuous *thunk-thunk* as the shafts whistled through his hands and struck their targets.

Johan was a blur of skill, eliciting encore after encore of applauded ovation. Billed above the Lion Tamer but below the Fire Eater, he was a wonder to behold. He had performed for kings and queens, emperors and despots, in every country on every map. Although his talents hadn't made him rich, they had made his name synonymous with excellence.

\* \* \* \*

The runaways and untimely deaths meant that Johan's nocturnal visits to Jack's caravan became more frequent. The catch on the door, the creak of footsteps on wooden boards, the swish of the blanket, the hot breath on the boy's neck. At first Jack had fought back, but Johan's sheer strength had overpowered him. What chance did a mere boy have against a grown man in the prime of physical condition?

He'd learnt to endure, biting his tongue, accepting Johan's love as an inescapable necessary evil. Where was he supposed to go? He had no home, no family. If he left the womb of the circus he would end up in an orphanage or worse: fighting for the Emperor on the eastern front. It was what it was.

Despite Johan's unsolicited attentions, life in the circus was good.  One big, happy travelling family.

* * * *

The finale was upon them, the crowd on the edge of their seats in anticipation of the final act.

*"Ladies and gentlemen, for your delectation and appreciation, a never-to-be-repeated performance by the incredible death-defying Johan. You will witness what those brave English souls at Agincourt wrought upon those mighty French. A sky darkened with arrows — death from above — no mercy and no escape. Brace yourself dear friends, for what you will witness is beyond belief!"*

Removing his cotton shirt, Johan prepared himself for the ordeal. Standing bare chested, arms wide in the center of the ring, he waited for the crowd to silence themselves.

*"Now!"* screamed the ringmaster.

In a choreographed deluge of steeled death, the javelins left the hands of the willing assistants above and hurtled towards the target below. Shaft after shaft intent on deadly contact sang toward the saw-dusted floor.

Gauging his moment, Jack stood up from the bench where he watched the performance. He knew how the trick worked. Two from the right, two from the left, followed by four down the center. A dance of death, the steps to which the public was not privy. He lifted his face and shouted her name.

* * * *

High above in the canopy, dressed in sequins and ostrich feathers, hung the young Katherine, a runaway, like himself, who'd found a home among the circus folk. Months of careful practice had taught her to count the steps in her head so that she knew exactly when to throw.

*One... two... three... throw.*

Simulated pitched chaos.

But tonight, her count was off. The javelin that should have gone left went right. She smiled down at Jack far below. They had each other. What could possibly go wrong?

\* \* \* \*

The shaft caught Johan in the eye, pierced his throat, passed through his abdomen, and neatly cleaved his penis, before burying itself into the clay floor of the ring. He never saw it coming, never felt the pain. Death was instantaneous. Like a pinioned marionette he hung, shafted, literally, in mid-stride.

The audience erupted.

Jack smiled up at Katherine.

Katherine smiled down at Jack.

# BLIGHTY

*France, a Somme trench, 1916...*

"SEEMS LIKE A HUNDRED years ago now, running down the High Street with the rest of the lads, leapfrogging our way down to the recruiters' station. The excitement and sense of impending adventure defining our life's purpose. I remember there were men and women standing in the streets, cheering and waving their miniature Union Jacks. Everybody was everybody's brother. There were no strangers in the town that day. We all knew somebody who was joining up, or someone who'd already joined. The king's shilling making kith and kin of us all. But that was back then, back home in Blighty. That was when we were just playing at war, rehearsing at being soldiers, perfecting bayonet lunges and parodying pain."

*The shell arced across no man's land, high above the wire and into the sky. It exploded above the trenches, drenching the subterranean world of the trench fighters in cold green light. Men shielded their eyes, protecting their night vision, the way they'd been taught at depot, before shipping out to France.*

"Cor blimey, how we used to complain but the sergeant was right; we never had it so bloody good. The whining was never ending - the beds too hard, the food rotten, liberty on Friday nights too short, the cost of a pint and the effort it took to kiss the pretty girls too much. Everything was a chore, an effort. Everything took too bloody long. Life was for living, and we were ready to live in the here and now, not the bloody future, not tomorrow, but now! We were ready alright, ready to shed our boyish ways and take up our manly responsibilities. Too eager by far to enjoy the warm beer at the bars, the frantic clinches in dark alleys, the jangle of shillings in our pockets. Looking back of course, now it don't seem so bad!"

*The flare dangled in the sky; the dark trail of smoke clearly visible against its luminescence. Drifting slowly to the ground, slipping through the air on the tiny parachute that held it aloft. As the flare fell the shadows grew and the largess of no man's land was reduced to pockets of pooled light and bottomless deep shadows. The flare fizzed, extinguishing itself in the puddled morass, the light still visible to cycloptic watchers the image burned deep into retinas.*

"But that was then, a lifetime ago when basic training was just a game. Army-issued passes invoking weekend freedoms; steam trains to distant nowheres to see friends and family before the great leap forward into France.

God, that train took forever, stopping at every bloody cattle call and whistle stop along the way! Took an age it did to cover the fifty miles from camp back to our village. We'd play cards or chat up one of the lasses, anything to kill the boredom. Many's the time we'd get off the train with a couple of extra quid in our pockets, Lady Luck having flashed her lovely smile. Wasn't always the case though, and sometimes we'd have to borrow a couple of shillings from Father till payday with some old flannel about paying him back later."

*Men who'd remained still when the flare hung high began to move about the trench. It was dangerous to move about when the flares were lit, the briefest of movements eliciting the whine of German bullets from the darkness beyond. Time slowed down, life came to a mud-sucking halt, the joy of spring recruitment now dead and buried in a richer part of Flanders Fields. The young who'd given up their youth now shambled like old ragged beggars, shuffling out their existence in the shit, where a day could last a week, a minute an entire lifetime.*

"Know what? Right now, I could really go for a pint of warm beer. I often find myself sitting on that train, between attacks and barrages — in my imagination of course — travelling back to our village, hoping upon hope that the journey takes forever, or at least just a while longer. Lounging back on those big horsehair cushions, no longer wishing life away. Enjoying the slow push and pull of steam, the corn in the fields, the smiles of the pretty girls."

*Somewhere in the distance an anonymous machine gun opens up, the mechanical chatter sowing death and injury on random trenches filled with anonymous faces. The bullets splash mud and blood. The dead and dying drop to the floor, the taste of muck in mouths, the smell of cordite in nostrils. Arse-clenching, piss-yourself fear seizing those still able to remember May Day recruitment.*

# DEAD STOP

*A desert road west of Phoenix, Arizona, 2011...*

THE VEHICLE LOST SPEED, brakes protesting as large rubber tires ground to a rolling halt. The truck stood at a four-way crossing. Nothing unusual about that except this time the stop was empty.

Fuel injected heat created a made-in-American mirage above the hood, faux flashing blues beguiling the casual observer. Burning desert sun glanced off paintwork, dazzling the driver, momentarily blinding as it danced on glass and sparkled on chrome. The driver squinted, adjusted the shade to block the glare and tugged his battered cap down over his eyes.

Prudence prevailing, he peered in all directions before gunning the engine and pulling away. The pride of hand-polished ownership vanished from view – the dust pall and exhausted-flatulence the only reminder it was ever there, that and a couple of air-sticking notes from some long-forgotten country legend. Summer-sunned wires hummed metallically, creeping grass whispered, black-top baked. Nothing exceptional, except this time the stop was empty.

The dirt-brown flats that passed for fields and margined the road were deserted, the cotton harvest gathered, the migrant workers presumably idle. Stop signs swayed, creaking in the gentle breeze, air whistling through the gunshot holes the local farm boys had blasted into them. A couple of birds sat on telegraph poles serenading what passed for traffic; a jackrabbit, the only other witness, disappeared into the undergrowth as quickly as it had appeared. A regular four-way stop, except this time it was empty.

Behind the tangled wire, next to the generic debris of cola cans and discarded industrial packaging stood a white cross. Memorial to eternity and everlasting life. There was a horseshoe at each of its stations; an ironic gesture considering the luck of the recipient. The arms were welded to the main upright, its white paint peeling, the rust blisters erupting in iron red flakes as the dry air ate it alive. Desert heat devoured everything eventually, including memorials to eternity and everlasting life.

Cobbled together by some grieving relative or well-meaning friend, the memorial stood in testimony to the once living, breathing corpse that now resided at Our Lady of Guadalupe on the far side of town. The marker, half-buried in long straw grass, memorialized the lives of previous visitors to the crossroads, belying the serenity of the scene – recalling a time when the crossing had been much busier than it was today.

*Gone were the blue probing lights, the wailing sirens and uniformed authority. No longer was the air rent with the cries and screams of urgency, the crunch of regulation footwear on broken glass. The ashes of traffic flares used to illuminate the car wreck had long since dispersed on dry desert breezes. Gone was the smell of spilt gasoline, burning rubber, the curious faces of nighttime passers pressed against darkened windows.*

*The only trace of the alcohol fueled birthday — celebrating the onset of manhood and the impossible prospect of youthful immortality — were the colored glinting jewels of gutter-strewn glass. Reminiscent of wreaths floating on distant oceans – memorializing the bodies of drowned sailors- the fragments reflected emotions past; mute to opinion, deaf to argument, screaming of a time when the crossroads hadn't been quite so pastoral.*

Brown tumble weed, paying no attention to the hazards of oncoming traffic and ignoring the protocol of motoring niceties, bustled through the four-way stop. Disappearing down the road, it raced towards some predestined rendezvous, leaving nothing but twigs and dust in its wake.

The sun began to wane. The wires twanged. The grass sighed, the heat of the day radiating as the earth gave up its warmth. It was just another day, nothing to write home about.

Except today, the stop was empty.

# VIOLATOR

*The local barbershop in downtown Phoenix,*
*Arizona, 2011...*

S O, IT'S HAIRCUT TIME again, the biweekly ritual where
I head out to my local barber and get the works.
Number-one cut on the back and sides, number-two
on top. I always leave the front a little longer. This helps
disguise the hereditary male-pattern thing. An exercise in
masturbation, a futile attempt to fool everybody apart from
myself! I always call it the *male-pattern thing* as mentioning
the *B-word* sends a *bed-pissing* shiver racing down my spine.

Don't know what it's all about really, the voluntary loss
of hair, but I always feel better for it. I compare it to one of
those born-again experiences, a cleansing ceremony, where I
walk in broken and come out whole. I always know when it's
time to go as the *fat fella* shows up in the mirror and makes
it painfully obvious that I've put on a bit of weight. Maybe
it's me, but there's something about a centimeter of erratic
stubbly grey growth that adds ten pounds to a bloke, or
perhaps I'm just kidding myself and I truly am the ballooned
gigantean that stalks my neighborhood?

Either way, after going through the motions and paying the
requisite fifteen bucks plus tip and tax, I always feel as though

I have completed my own personal twelve-step program, that I'm well on my way to a life of guiltless fat-free, slim-lined fitness. Illusions of Jenny Craig calling me up, asking me to be her poster boy — hate mail from Jared afraid of competition and losing his lucrative deal at the sandwich shop.

Normally I go during the week when the barbershop isn't so busy. A simple case of grabbing a chair, flicking through the magazines, and waiting for the invitation to take my place in one of the high leather swivel chairs on the operations floor.

The magazines are always the same — outdated, dog-eared, and over-read. I say over-read, however, if the rest of the clientele are like me then they just nose through the covers and look at the pictures, browsing through ads that try to convince me that, despite my crappy desperate day job, I can afford a Ferrari-Gucci lifestyle.

Comparing myself, as I finger through the pages, to the six-packed studs, convinced that all it would take to look just like them would be a supreme effort on my part - that an occasional visit to the local gym.

I always linger on the bikini shots — ogling the beach-dusted, suntanned beauties. It's not exactly pornography — I mean they're in regular magazines, not one of those top-shelf cellophane-sealed publications filled with semi-legitimate stories on World War One aircraft and suggestions on how to super-charge your lawn mower. Even so, the *nice girls* are working their hardest to squirm out of every inch of cloth, their bikini straps hanging loose, their bottoms pulled so far down little fantasy is required to imagine the last couple inches of forbidden flesh.

But this week instead of going during the week I end up going on Saturday, household chores and marital necessity forcing me to forgo my ritual and put my time on hold for an extra twenty-four hours. Responsibilities fulfilled I break free from my institutional obligations and head down to the barbershop.

The car park is full; I know this is going to be a pain. The chairs in the waiting area are bound to be taken and the only magazines left will be the gardening weeklies and the women's supplements that have somehow managed to slip between the muscle mags and this year's swimwear editions.

Don't get me wrong, Lindsay Lohan and her ilk interest me as much as the next bloke, but there's only so much one can take.

From the check-out lines in the supermarket, to the Hollywood insider TV shows, I'm bombarded with nearly famous nobodies living coke-dependent Californian lifestyles. After a while all the exposure to wealth and decadence tends to make me feel inadequate and passed over. Very clearly, I am missing out!

I walk towards the door. Can't really see inside as they've put that dark film across the windows, giving the place an air of *dubiousness*, cloaking the clientele in shaded mystery. However, the one thing that is clearly visible, a sign that even a blind man wouldn't have trouble seeing from the other side of the car park, is the red and white spinning pole. There's something about it — almost phallic in its appearance — an autoerotic symbol only truly appreciated by men. It seems to scream "Come in you manly men!" Banishing females and their feminine ways from the man only buffet of manliness inside. To my surprise, apart from a couple of dads waiting for sons, the chairs are empty; young boys receiving initiation rites into barbershop ritual, an experience they will carry with them for the rest of their lives;- new warriors to fill the gaps of the fallen, shouldering the burden of the few and the brave, taking their place alongside those of the greatest generation. The older war-horses who, through no fault of their own have died off, or are so addled with age, can no longer make it to the service.

'Cos that is what it is. Getting your hair cut is a religious experience. The acolytes in their white coats, the silver chalices filled with Aqua Velva, and the Holy Rood symbolized in crossed scissors, wielded with devotion and dexterity by the priests of partings. No hymns, no prayers, just pure supplication, the feeling that you have encountered something greater than yourself. Yes, a feeling of being at one with God in his universe.

A church maybe, but not exactly a confessional, although Manuel, who normally cuts my hair, knows everything about me — my wife's name, the kids' sports, how much I hate my job, and my Tuesday morning dalliance with the MILF from number thirty-six. It's not like he is going to tell anyone — I mean its information shared — quid pro quo! I tell him, he tells me. A little dirt, and before you know it, we're chatting like long-lost brothers.

It's no secret that me and Manuel have a lot in common -- on some things. The fact is he likes redheads and I like brunettes — he likes butts and I'm more of a boob man. Those differences we have in common. Subjects near and dear to our hearts that keep us chatting for hours. That's what I like about our little chats, the profound conversations, the difficult topics we choose not to avoid. But it isn't always talk, it isn't always fun and games. Sometimes we say nothing at all. Not in the oppressive, silent, uncomfortable sort of way you might think. We'll chat away and then we'll drift into silence as Manuel concentrates on his craft, and I give myself over totally to the ultimate experience - putting the reins in some ones else's hands for a change -- handing over the helm to a different captain.

So, there I am sitting on my leather-cushioned throne, glimpsing image after image of myself in the eternal mirrors, watching some generic football game on television. I spend a couple of seconds of my life trying to recognize the teams and ask Manuel in my deepest voice what the score is, pretending that I really care. Both antagonists are from the colleges that I never attended and so I ignore his heavily accented, recently border-crossed English.

A new customer sits down opposite me, and I feel the draft from the sheet the barber wafts across the knees of the fresh inductee. Like white sail cloth the sheet billows up in the air. Quite beautiful when you think about it! Nothing unusual though, I've seen Pedro's flourish a hundred times. However, on this one occasion I stare. The customer opposite stares back so I quickly look away. You know the manly thing? Pretending to ignore each other even though we're both perfectly aware of what just happened? I take a sneaky look out of the corner of my eye, faking a look at one of the myriad examples of faux barbershop ephemera. You know the stuff I mean, the sepia photographs of mustached men from the 1930s dressed in white aprons; advertisements for no longer manufactured shaving salves and safety razors.

### The person opposite me is a woman!

I know, I can hardly believe it myself. Shocked and stunned I was a female! Surely, she knows this is where the men come? Don't they have their own special places with their own special kinds of service? Beauty parlors and nail salons, massage parlors and Brazilian waxing studios? Given the multitude of choices, I had to ask myself what it was she possibly want here, and besides that, who had given her permission? Surely there has to be some kind of Papal dispensation before the opposite sex is allowed to enter the temple! Of course, I'm a little pissed, a bit annoyed — hot under the collar you might say.

The woman opposite me is a black female with short, tight, dark curly hair. I hear her speaking to one of my confessors and by the sounds of things she is looking for a shave. No, not the kind where they press you with warm towels, apply copious amounts of shaving cream and then drag an instrument of death across your face, leaving you whisker free for at least two days — the head kind of shave! She wants her hairline shaved up, to give her one of those Nubian princess looks. The kind you've seen in *National*

*Geographic* on the bust of Queen Nefertiti, high and tight, accentuating the strong African brow and the crease of her skull.

So now I've experienced it — didn't think I ever would. I mean I've heard a diamond ring and seen a dragon fly, as the song goes, but never have I seen a woman in a barber's chair. I mumble something to Manuel, who mumbles back, clicking his tongue in disgust. Now I've got a story to tell. My humdrum life has just gotten interesting - just as I thought life had peaked and the buzzer had blasted for the end of the final period and the gauge had exploded on the interest scale, things went from mild to worse.

Miss Nubian across the way from me pulls out a pink smart phone, uncrosses her legs and proceeds to press the digits. Her barber stops, thinking that it must be something urgent, but she waves a manicured hand, indicating for him to go on. I'm not sure who is more shocked, me or Manuel's buddy? How the hell are you supposed to cut someone's hair when their hand is glued to the side of the head? Unperturbed and demonstrating his sheer professionalism, Pedro, with desert-hopping precision, carries on. His scissors whip around her hand-held phone without even nipping her. Not a trace of blood in the blur of hair and steel!

My time is done, my hair is perfect, and I am good to go. Manuel walks me to the till, offers me something for the weekend and then thanks me for the totally unexpected five-dollar tip I give him every other week. He slaps me on the back, wishes me a fantastic rest of my day and then jinxes my team by wishing them good luck. My moment in the barber shop is done.

I catch my reflection in the window, admire how square my jaw looks and notice my new slim-line figure. Happy with the cut and satisfied with the copious amounts of aftershave wafting around me, I shake my head and wring my hands in disbelief. It's not that my experience was totally ruined, it's just that I feel a little violated, a little damaged.

## A female in a barber shop. The nerve of the woman!

I can get over the haircut, even the shave, as time eventually cures all. Every woman needs an occasional spit and polish, a little personal pretty time, but making phone calls during the devotional on a pink phone!

That's going a tad too far, and no doubt will take me a lifetime to get over!

# IN MEMORIAM —
# ODE TO A GRANDFATHER

*Every timeless memory...*

O N THE OTHER SIDE of the ocean, in a country I like
to call my own, rests a man quite still and at peace.
Mourned by family and friends in a room filled
with empty teacups, half-eaten sandwiches, and hushed
conversation. Where soft tissue dabs at cruel tears and
laughter ripples into fond remembrance. Murmured voices
change painful subjects, as the subject himself listens with
deaf ears. Gone the worries, the pains and complaints, gone
the insurmountable stairs.

Larger than life, a man who greedily lived his own ten
times over, now lies compacted and crated in pine. A colossus
who bestrode the world, shielded family and defended
Empire, now resigned to a cold churchyard plot. Final prayers
and sad farewells — forced to endure the poignant tone of
Last Post and the whisper of unfurling flags.

Now we talk of the man in the past tense when only
yesterday we were complaining bitterly in the present. The
sacrifice required of loved ones who can barely take care of
themselves let alone care for the sick and infirm. How if
only's and what ifs were replaced with adequate facilities and

shorter hospital waiting lists — wishes that would enable beggars to ride. Those concerns are gone now, substituted with funeral arrangements and timetables, telephone calls and whispered voices. *What's best for Jack? What would Jack want that's best for us?* A man available to all, now fitting his afterlife into our busy schedules.

Not exactly a knight on a white steed, more a welcome flat-capped face on a squeaking, rusting bicycle. Scalded for dirty boots and errant household ways, he'd endure the wrath of marital bliss, accepting blame for things he hadn't done. If the Japs couldn't get him what chance did his wife and kids have of scratching that tough exterior? An armor-plated veteran in slippers and a cardigan, the epitome of Englishness, a son of Yorkshire — an inspiration to us all.

Grandfather, uncle, husband, father and friend — a man who answered to many names. A multitasking genius and juggler of renown; a jack of all trades, who'd seen it, been it and bought the holiday home. A man who could weave a tale like no other, talk the hind legs off a donkey and yet there were some stories he wouldn't tell. Stories alluded to by the blue-black ink on shrapnel'ed hands that would remain with him forever. Briefly shared but never explained, an outburst of emotion and a flood of tears — a softer side to a man of steel.

Gone but not forgotten. Nature abhors a vacuum but the space he occupied will be hard to fill. The house will hold him forever and our hearts are fuller for having known him. The empty chair by the television, chocolate bars in the fridge, and the myriad pill bottles he refused to open.

"Bloody doctors, what do they know anyway?" What did they know about healing a man broken on the inside? What did they know about plugging a heart the size of a planet? Advice taken but wisely ignored.

A soldier who's gone on to greater things — standing to attention in Elysium's pantheon. No longer in a world carved by bullet and bomb, but one turfed and flowered, treed and hedged. A place fit for heroes and dead grandfathers. A warm welcome from comrades passed. A seat by the home fire and a welcome brew. Now he can rest that pack and throw down the rifle that need never be fired again.

"What took you so long Jack? We've been waiting for you forever!"

"I was busy lads. Stuff to do and family to look after, you know... Can't just run away and leave it for others now, can you?"

Knowing smiles and nudges.

Aye, that's the Jack they remembered. Bloody hero is our Jack.

Don't hear that much in these days of reality drivel, where a man stands out for his qualities rather than the way he looks in name-branded shoes on the front page of some random gossip magazine.

A man's man, a woman's man, a family man. A man to be remembered and to emulate.

Dear Jack, I've dried my tears and mended my heart but the hole you've created in a life a thousand miles from where you lie will be hard to fill. The red barrier tape and flashing lights that surround the crater you have left will serve as memorial, where the very depth of memory echoes in the pitch blackness of our recent loss.

Memories of a man who cried upon arrivals and goodbyes, who held one transfixed with his one good eye.

I love you Jack.

Goodnight, Sweet Prince.

# NORTH EASTERN PROMISE

*Not at every Christmas...*

G EORGE RUBBED HIS HANDS together and sucked on his dentures. Getting old was a bastard and something he really didn't appreciate. The doc had told him that he needed to get away, find some blue sky and palm trees, but there was fat chance of that. With a wife to support on an ex-coalminer's pension they weren't exactly living large. Thirty-five years he'd spent down the pit; man and boy giving his life for the black stuff. What else could he have done? His dad had been a miner and his grandfather before him, so for his thirteenth birthday he received a pair of steel-toed boots and a permission slip to leave school early. A brown paper envelope with a couple of quid at the end of the week was far more important to the family than a leaving certificate. Higher education was for posh folk.

George coughed and tasted blood in his mouth. He was in his sixties, but you would easily have given him seventy. The problem with working down the pit was that it took as much from you as you took out of it. The more coal, the more aches and pains. With slipped discs, rheumatism, grating joints, stone lung and a lazy eye, he'd paid the price and was more than thankful when they'd finally retired him. He'd just about bitten the pit manager's hand off when he'd been presented with his gold watch and thanked for his years of service. Put out to grass like some old knackered horse, to enjoy the last years of his life stumbling around his vegetable patch and getting under his wife's feet. Big gardener was George, took good care of his council allotment — nobody grew onions like him. The secret was pigeon shit, but people didn't need to know that!

His long-suffering wife would watch him through condensed panes as he pottered around the back yard, mindful of the strong, virulent virile man he'd once been. The pit had crushed him like a bug, and she couldn't remember the last time they'd been physical. Loved him to death though, even if he was a cantankerous old fart. Liked his own way did George, but Mary made sure he didn't always get it.

For Christmas, the kids bought him a greenhouse, one of those modular all-year-round, bio-thermal units. Aluminum framed with special glass that would attract more UV rays and help the plants to flourish; at least that's what the description claimed in the catalogue. They'd clubbed together and, with a fortuitous win at the Friday night bingo, had enough to pay the thing off in twenty-seven easy installments.

Strange looking thing. It was like a crushed egg with a pyramid-shaped top. Designed ergonomically to ensure the maximum utilization of the space within.

Christmas had come and gone, and they'd hired a couple of strapping lads to help erect it in the back yard. They'd placed it out on the cobbles where the old wooden shed had stood. George had seen his wife eye the young lads sweating in the afternoon sun — he wasn't jealous, just cognizant that age and infirmity spared no one. Now the greenhouse was full of tomatoes, peppers and various other greenery not indigenous to the Yorkshire countryside.

George loved the gift and from the very beginning went to work preparing his seed beds and perfecting his irrigation. The watery north eastern sun radiating through the polarized glass felt good on his body as he toiled in the dirt and there was definitely a lessening of the ache in his joints. After working all day beneath the glass, and sitting in his comfy chair of an evening, sleep came easily. Mary noticed a lifting of his mood and even commented on the extra spring in his step; it was good to see a man who'd worked hard all his life enjoying his final years.

George was amazed at the crops that flourished beneath the glass. He'd never seen tomatoes like them; giant, red brutes that burst with juice and flavor. Even the onions he prided himself on were larger and tastier and he no longer had to use the pigeon manure, although it'd been a hard habit to break.

During show season he took first prize in nearly every category, something nobody in the town had ever done. The judges admired his bounty and his fellow competitors, green with envy, patted him on the back and congratulated him. What was his secret, and would he share? George just tapped his soil-stained finger against the side of his nose and smiled noncommittally. "Now then lads," he said, "a gentleman never kisses and tells."

Truth be told, he was a little baffled himself as he wasn't the only gardener in the area with a greenhouse; some of the other old boys had them too, and yet their produce, although fantastic, didn't come close to his. His veg seemed to grow twice as quick, twice as large, and twice as tasty. George put it down to his green thumb; his rivals put it down to devious practices and cried foul play behind his back.

Sitting in front of the telly one evening, the fire blazing and with fish and chips in newspaper on his lap, George watched some random program on the BBC. He wouldn't watch ITV (hated the adverts!) out of principal and there was horse jumping on the other channel, so he was stuck with whatever Aunty Beeb was showing. Some documentary about Egypt and the pyramids; alien technology and conspiracy theories. All very well, he thought, as he shoveled a couple of soggy chips into his mouth, the salt and vinegar biting into his lips. A man in khaki, wearing a pith helmet, was enthusiastically remonstrating about the power of the pyramids — how he believed that they were ancient energy sources, not just tombs as mainstream Egyptologists would have us believe.

Obviously, the fella was a nutter, thought George, but it would kill an hour before he went up to bed. The presenter went onto describe propagation theory, how plants placed within the ancient structures would flourish, generating abundant harvests. It was also believed that the energy within the chambers had medicinal properties, and that the ancients had used the pyramids for their healing properties.

"Codswallop!" spluttered George through battered haddock and mushy peas.

For a brief instant, light swept through the front room as scudding clouds revealed a reluctant moon — the fleeting beams glanced off the greenhouse at the bottom of the garden.

George gulped. "Bloody hell," he cursed under his breath.

"George love," called Mary, "I'm going up to bed. See you in a bit?"

"Right-o lass. I'll just finish me scran and I'll be up."

His greenhouse was an effing pyramid! No wonder the vegetables were doing so well. It was ancient Egyptian technology that was causing his onions to expand at such an enviable rate.

George wasn't a big believer in coincidence but the titles running up the television screen on the rear end of a retreating camel seemed to be screaming out to him. Maybe they were bloody right. Maybe there was something in it. He wondered if, just maybe, they were right about the other stuff as well.

George finished his dinner and then sat through a program on political affairs, almost falling asleep himself until he heard the soft snores of his wife emanating from the upstairs bedroom.

It was worth a shot. What did he have to lose?

He grabbed a blanket from the airing cupboard, a thermos filled with cocoa from the kitchen, and as quietly as possible stole from the house. Careful to make as little noise as possible, he headed out into the yard. It was cold outside, but he felt warmth emanate from the greenhouse as he slid open the glass door. He'd obviously gone off his rocker. Folk would think he was bonkers, but it was worth a try. He'd already noticed a change in his temperament and friends and family had commented on how well he was looking. Even the squeak in his dodgy knee had somehow been lubricated and disappeared. He settled himself into an old deck chair, wrapped the blanket around himself, and with the odor of warm soil and ripening tomatoes in his nostrils, drifted into sleep.

\* \* \* \*

Mary came down the stairs and entered the living room. She'd woken up alone, which wasn't unusual, as George would often fall asleep in front of the telly. She'd find him fully dressed and unconscious in the big comfy chair – the television playing to an inattentive audience. She walked towards where she expected to find her husband, but the chair was empty. Now she was worried. George never went anywhere without telling her first and even then, those occasions were few and far between. She walked into the kitchen, called out his name, but there was no reply. Where could he be? It wasn't like him. She eyed the telephone hanging on the wall, thought about calling the police and then dismissed the idea as silly. Where could he be? He couldn't have gone far.

She peered through the kitchen window, out to where George's pride and joy stood. Surely not she thought, but it was worth a try. Given the recent success he'd enjoyed at the local horticultural show she wouldn't put it past the old fool. She shuffled her feet into her slippers, pulled her nightgown around her, opened the back door and went down the garden. Silly old bugger! What did he think he was playing at, scaring her like that? She'd give him what for.

"George? George are you out here?" she called. Nothing except the clink of the electric milk float as it rattled past out on the road, but no sign of George. She walked towards the greenhouse and slid open the door. She was getting nervous now, a little afraid of what she might find. He may be half lame and blind in one eye, but he certainly wasn't deaf.

Mary screamed.

Slumped in a chair was her George, a look of serenity covering his face.

My God, not George! Surely not her George? Not like this. Not now!

Mary's scream caused George to shoot up out of this chair.

"Bloody hell woman, what the hell are you doing? You half scared me to bleeding death. Are you trying to collect on the life insurance or somat?"

Mary stood in front of her husband, one hand over her mouth, the other pointing towards him.

"What is it lass? What's wrong?"

Mary couldn't believe her eyes. It was George alright, large as life but not the George she'd said goodnight to. The man in front of her was buff and ripped; his toned physique bulged through an unbuttoned shirt. His hair was thick and dark and there was the twinkle in both his eyes that had caused her to fall in love with him those thirty-odd years ago. It was as though he'd lost years. Shocked by the man who stood in front of her she felt her knees buckle beneath her.

George, still not understanding what was going on, caught her as she fell, gathered her up in his massive arms and carried her back to the house. Neglecting to take off his boots, he pushed open the kitchen door, walked through to the living room and laid her on the couch. As he stood up, he caught his reflection in the mirror above the fireplace, or rather the reflection of the man he'd once been.

"Flippin Nora!" he gasped out loud. How was he going to explain this to the lads down at the working men's club? This was going to be slightly more difficult than giant onions and pigeon poop!

# AN ODE TO CURRY

*Seems like yesterday...*

> *"It is a truth universally acknowledged that an Englishman in possession of a couple of quid and a belly full of beer must be in want of a curry..."*
>
> **~ Jane Austen, Pride and Prejudice ~**

O
H, SWEET ELIXIR OF life, the meaning of reason, and the object of my desire. What it is to be bereft of thy company, only to rekindle joyous acquaintance in my unhappy hour of want? Words cannot quantify nor does allusion describe the bitter-sweet of fond, empty-plated remembrance. Clothed in plastic-bagged-fantastic and foiled in silver, thou art a joy to behold; a breath of fresh, pungent air, a tangible tingle to the nostrils, a veritable mistress of saucy delight. A jewel to the eye, a sear to the soul and a burning rush of requited love. Solitary, confined moments shared and savored where one can reflect and revisit the intimacy of oral delight. Never was there a less selfish lover — never were the clinging moments more cherished — never was one left so bereaved by flushed adieu. Until we eat again, I bid thee a flatulent farewell!

* * * *

"Last orders ladies and gentlemen, please!" screams the potbellied publican from behind faux teak and poor dentistry. Standing amidst an island of factory-produced nostalgia, he checks his watch and rings the bell one last time. "Come on now, move your arses! Ain't you got homes to go to?"

I finish the suds in my glass, choking back the stagnant liquid that just moments before browsed golden as it bubbled and foamed, and place it on the countertop with the other dead soldiers. Pint and shot glasses stand together in blissful union, unaware their usefulness has passed, and that closing time has robbed them of employment. I look around at my fellow imbibers and through alcohol-addled eyes, spy the lonely and the loved as they file through the exit and into to the icy embrace of life. Their moments of communal pain-dulling congenial inebriation now forgotten as they check wallets, grab jackets and fondle newfound soul mates.

The weekend is over, and the morning brings another day at the foundry, office or other unworthy place of forced employment. Wage slaved to the boss, the credit card, and the mortgage; they scuttle to grab precious hours of sleep before the onslaught of fresh corporate demands engulf them.

I consider making a move on the last female at the bar but realize before I engage in optimistic social intercourse that either from want or neglect, there's probably a reason she's still there. I rethink my strategy, drag myself from my wooden throne, and trudge into the night.

It's cold outside and I spy my reflection in the puddles of monsoon-ravaged Middle England. Despite the chill there's prospective inner warmth, the knowledge that only mere yards away lays a harbor of tranquility — a safe haven in an otherwise harsh, unforgiving world. I smell it before I see it;

my feet splashing through water, my heels clicking on the pavement as unseen, aromatic hands grab me by the shirt collar, slap me about the face and drag me towards their irresistible event horizon. The choice isn't my own, it's a necessity, survival instinct; an innate sense of following one's nose and complying with one's inner hunter-gatherer.

I stand before the plate glass window, the light from the restaurant transfixing me with its hypnotic tractor beam. There's no escape, no use running — the dinner bell has sounded, and like a Pavlovian puppy I salivate into my jacket.

The House of Bombay; it might as well be the Church of the Holy Sepulcher, the final resting place of the Holy Grail, or the gates of Valhalla. I grin moronically, my eyes wide with anticipation, my tongue thickening in my mouth at the prospect of what I am about to receive. I am truly grateful, and I push open the door and enter paradise on earth. It isn't a religious revelation but I'm sure the Buddhists and Taoists would recognize the spiritual transformation I am experiencing. Truly one of the converted, my faith unshakeable, I accept the dogma completely and throw myself before my altar of expectation.

The restaurant is full of excited voices and exotic smells, its tables occupied by like-minded individuals who've escaped the pub and stopped for a bite on their way home, a perfect ending to a perfect night. Ten pints of lager, a bag of crisps, a game of grab ass on the dance floor, all washed down with lashings of the hot and spicy.

**"...These are the things. These are the things.**
**The things that dreams are made of..."**
**The Human League**

What to choose, what to choose? The delicacies of the great Indian sub-continent are catalogued before me in a cornucopia of delectation and gastronomic delight. A temptation to the weak, a fix to the addicted, but a delight to the enlightened. The crash of pots and pans and the mantra of cursed Urdu transport me to a place far from windswept, rain-soaked, Yorkshire. No longer the last man at the bar but a willing supplicant at the place of pilgrimage. An acolyte shoves a much-fingered menu into my hands and demands to know what I'm drinking. Being the connoisseur that I am, I choose an Indian beer that claims to have been brewed on the banks of the river Ganges. *National Geographic* images waft through my mind as I briefly swim through the corpses and crocodiles to the sari-ed beauty that holds a bottle outstretched in her henna-ed hand.

I grasp, I sip, I swallow.

Reacting to the broken English of the waiter, I flick through the curled pages of the stained menu and peruse the delights of the Punjab, the Kashmir, the snowcapped peaks of the Himalayas, and the golden sands of the Southern Keralan coastline.

Lamb or beef, chicken or shrimp, veggies or not?

The aromas are intense, the Bollywood music blaring, the Indian chatter emanating from the kitchen incessant. Having made my choice, I shut the menu. Poised with pen in hand, the sauce-splattered waiter prepares to notate my desire.

"Vindaloo, so bloody hot that it'll burn my arse. Don't forget the naan or the poppadum's and jump to it Gupta! I'm bloody starving."

The waiter smiles, he's heard it all before, the well-meant racial slurs roll off his back like a rice-paddied buffalo flicking flies. He beams his gold-toothed smile and moves quickly behind the counter and disappears through the hanging colored beads into the kitchen. The bastard will make me pay for my flippant comments and no doubt there will be more than just chili powder in my tinfoil take-away box — a huge dose of scotch bonnet pepper, a little liquid napalm perhaps. It will be Gupta's name that I scream in abject agony the morning after the night before.

Cold hard cash clinks from my sweaty palm and the mutually beneficial exchange is made. A silver container, already oozing brown joy, exchanged for a couple of dirty notes — the pleasure is all mine, although judging by the grin on my newfound friend's face the pleasure is all his. I walk to the door and make my exit.

As I trudge through the rain, I reflect on the wisdom of ignoring the femme fatale at the bar. The last girl in the world, at least on this particular Friday night, shunned for the illicit pleasure of liquid love — I hate to share and besides, Gupta only gave me one plastic fork.

C'est la vie baby, maybe next time.

**"...Club Tropicana's drinks are free.**
**Fun and sunshine — there's enough for everyone..."**
**~ Wham**

# PERFECT SKY

*Timeless...*

Blue blown and sky chased, the puff-gusted halcyon
of summer longs.

With soft, splashed shape, nimbus hangs fresh
breathed and heaven braced.

Buoyant — steepled, storeyed,
stacked with soft crush.

The easy ooze of liquid light, the gentle creep
of summer hush.

Scattered like cushions, the blinding sapphire
of glassed forever

Submits to dapple-daubed shadow.
The brushed caress of Westings past.

# EPILOGUE

*The eternity of pen in hand...*

THE TIME HAS COME, the writ is wrote; chimed memory, which fell so deftly on the recently attentive, now echoes in deaf ears. A new year, a great leap forward, a procession of majesty and literary uncertainty.

## Will this be the year?

Will the loose leaves of accumulated cobbled wisdom and un-championed prose attain their rightful place on the podium of publication? Will the fire-wrought chapters Black Panther-punch their way into the limelight, or will they forever gleam dully from behind the mists of what might have been's and Anglo-elitist mediocrity? A forgotten script dipped in the dust of malcontent and micro rewrites; the hope and expectation of nonspecific comments coupled with cyber-spaced applause — sleeve-worn expectation on - a blog to nowhere?

I have it, I know it — I've been told time and again. My words bound from the page, my metaphors meteoric, my spelling less than desirable. But the genus of originality all pervasive. Short stories created with an even shorter attention span; tweaked and pared to perfection, cobbled and honed, whittled and scrimshawed.

But for a sign — a skywritten indication — a helio-flashed glimmer of recognition from the ivory towers on the rim of possibility. To cross swords just once with the illuminati of literary immortality.

**Just one line-tugging bite as I prepare to my cast my hook into the pool of uncertainty, hopeful that my sparkling tin fish is noticed and gobbled down as it trims and dazzles, darts and dives.**

Endless cups of tea coupled with quotidian-blinkered perusals of the web-connected. Another day of energetic scribblings margined by the angst of colonial miscomprehension. Worried, terrified, and scared, of not achieving the achievable. It's out there, I can smell it — hear it screaming my name. The beast that abounds in the forest of library shelves demanding my tribute — begging for my submission. I can feel its vibration through the tracks, see it ripple across a pond; sense it in the boughs of breeze-blown trees. The time is right, the manuscript is now.

Expectations of an adoring public, the *oohs and aahs* of generic acclaim as I climb, explode and scintillate. The moment forever scorched into the retinas of men — a brief illumination, a sweet remembrance of a life lived and not forgotten. Immortality attained through the medium of wood pulp and India ink.

The year when dragons are chased back into the forest, banners flapping from castellated grandeur, battle cries echoing from ancient stones.

**Come on you bastards. Come and bloody get me!**

# THE AUTHOR

COLIN JAMES, AN ENGLISHMAN who emigrated to the U.S. in 2001, is a happy man with two terrible children. After various junctures in New Mexico and New York, he and his family are now settled in Arizona. The career path he has followed has taken him from the ranks of the British Army to the tops of Austrian mountains as a ski guide.

A student of English literature, he has been published in several online literary magazines including *THE FRONT PORCH* and *AT THE BIJOU*. His work has appeared in print in *THE STARVING ARTIST* and he has received accolades from several prestigious writing competitions.

A rising literary star, his first novel **LORD ALF** is due to be published in Fall 2020 by Cresting Wave Publishing, LLC.